BLOOD & SPURS
A TOURNAMENT LIKE NO OTHER

A Western Novella
By Mark Tarrant

Edited by Chris Gruber

Cover Featuring Actors:
Clint Hummel
Adam Chess & James Blackburn
View them in action at
www.BloodAndSpurs.com

Based on the screenplay
Blood and Spurs.
By Mark Tarrant

From the Author

I always wanted to write a western tale with characters from so many walks of life. Growing up, I read very few westerns but watched so many western films. Yes, Clint Eastwood is my favourite western movie actor and Josey Wales had some of the greatest lines ever in a film.

I originally wrote *Blood and Spurs* as a script and tried to make a film with very talented people in New Mexico, but it was not in the cards at that time. Be sure to watch the trailer at BloodAndSpurs.com. I thought the story was fun, and I hope I did the story justice in writing the novella based on the screenplay.

I hope you enjoy this western tale. Thanks for taking the time to look at my imagination's work set in the beautiful state of New Mexico.

Let's ride amigos!

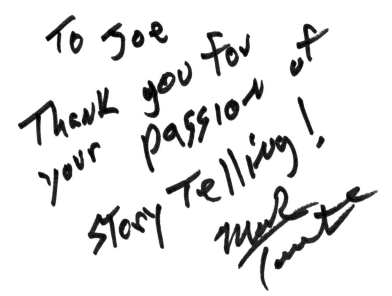

To you

Thank you for it
your passion
Story telling !

Chapter 1

It was not only her beauty, not only her smile but the way she laughed at his jokes that weren't funny. He loved her. She had been so beautiful, with a smile that brightened every room she entered. But now, the life drained from her once vibrant face as she clung to his rigid body. She looked into his bewildered eyes, and he could tell she was fading fast. He felt lost.

Her strong grasp on his shoulders weakened as she slid to the floor. Blood poured from her chest, soaking her long, yellow dress. Jack swallowed hard, looking up at the judge. The judge was in his early sixties. He was worn, rugged but regal. He stood motionless with the same look in his eyes. The two men locked gazes. She crumpled to the floor; a jolt of awareness that he just made the biggest mistake of his life coursed through his veins.

Confusion quickly turned to anger. The judge straightened his gun with a shaky grip and pulled the trigger. Jack was quick as he ducked, the sound echoing in the doorway as he rolled and lunged through the front door. He managed to get a couple of steps away before two more shots rang out. This time, he felt a burning pain pierce his thigh. He stumbled down the stairs. The power of fear and the rush of adrenalin gave the young man the strength to stagger away from the judge's home.

The maddened judge stood on the porch, lining up another shot. Jack pulled his pistol and shot back over his shoulder, hoping to distract him. He continued firing blindly, causing the judge to pause and step back into the doorway for cover. Gritting his teeth, the judge took aim and fired three more shots, but he only struck air. He watched the young, blond-haired man disappear into the nearby trees. Looking down the porch, he saw a wet trail of blood drops leading down the steps. He had hit the son of a bitch. Now he would have to hunt him like a wounded animal.

"Daddy… daddy," the dying girl whimpered. Blood trickled from her soft pink lips.

The judge ran back inside to his daughter who lay bleeding out on the Oriental rug. He tossed the gun aside and fell to his knees, scooping his only child in his arms.

"I'm here sweetheart, I'm here," he said with a cracking voice.

"Daddy … why?" she asked.

"I am sorry … I …"

She smiled weakly and then shuddered as the last bit of life drained from her body. She was gone. Her eyes faded like a candle blown out in a short breeze. The judge began to weep.

"I'll fix this. I'll find a way. I'll find him, and no one will know. I am so sorry … I have to fix this. It's his fault. He was going to take you away from me. Why did you hide your relationship from me? That bastard will pay. It's his fault; this is all his fault!"

The judge lowered his daughter to the floor and picked up his revolver. He ran to the front door, looking out at the emptiness of the dirt road. With watery eyes, he tried to scan the fields and tree line.

"I'll find you. You will pay … you son of a bitch. I'll carve out your heart!" he screamed.

Just a half-mile away, Jack could hear the threats in the distance. He kept running, though now with a hobble, darting between rocks and small trees. His leg swelled with pain. He only looked back briefly to think of her, remembering their plans. Maybe she was still alive. Maybe it wasn't as bad as it looked … or maybe he was going to have to keep running for his life. He stopped and bent over, taking several deep breaths. He looked at the gun still clenched in his bloody, twitching hands. He shook his head and took off running again.

Chapter 2

The sun was setting over the small mountain ranges of southern New Mexico. An adobe church, surrounded by desert shrubs and prickly cacti, sat alone in the wilderness. This small church building housed a few souls, one of whom was very lost. Charlie Blackburn sat outside on a weathered barrel, watching the sun go down. He thumbed through a large Bible, his blue eyes scanning the pages. He paused to squint up at the sun every few moments. He wore a priestly robe and a large wooden cross, which hung from a leather string around his neck. Feeling uninspired, he closed the Bible and lowered his head.

"Sometimes, the book isn't what ya need," came a voice.

Charlie looked over his shoulder to see a priest with a balding head and a scarred left cheek leaning in the doorway.

"Oh, I'm sure whatever ails me is in here somewhere. That's what you fellas have been trying to help me find since you took me in."

Charlie stood up and stretched. He looked at Brother Ramirez. Rugged, cunning, and confident like an old wolf, Brother Ramirez was a free spirit amongst the brothers at the church of San Philippe. There's always a wild card in every group, and brother Ramirez was it. He had seen a good deal of war and revolution, though the others asked him to keep his past to himself. Charlie didn't mind. He preferred an honest, straight shooter than someone who hid the truth to spare your feelings.

"You've been here almost a year, but the last few weeks amigo, you ain't been here at all," Ramirez said.

"Ghosts," Charlie answered. "Just ghosts from the past."

Ramirez grinned and rubbed his jaw.

"Well, you got some Biblical education, helped with the local villages and made a few friends. Maybe it's time to find a flock."

Charlie laughed.

"I ain't in no shape to lead men again, especially to the good Lord."

"Well, you won't know until you try," Ramirez said.

"I ain't a preacher. I ain't a leader. And right now, I don't know what I am."

"I know you ain't no preacher, you're just horrible at it. I was trying to be nice, but I know if you stay here thinking you can change who and what you are by hiding from the world, you'll never get rid of those ghosts."

Biting his lip, Charlie shook his head.

Ramirez continued, "I know, son, been there. War is brutal, and with all the killing and fighting, it brings out the darkest side of a man. But you need to get back into the world. You are too young and too smart to hide for the rest of your life. And anyway, you're the worst preacher I've seen in ten years."

"That's some encouragement," Charlie mumbled.

Brother Ramirez stepped from the church entranceway, grabbing Charlie by the robe and swiftly pulling him around the church wall. He pinned him against the building as Charlie tried to break his grasp on his robe. He was strong for an old wolf.

"Okay, now listen you sorry son of a bitch, you won't get better until you leave this place. You needed shelter and guidance. You needed the Lord, but now you need to get back and get on with life. I am old. I've lived. I outlived two wives, and I have no children. I do what I can here. I like the brothers and the villages, but you need to go. You need to find yourself again. Don't end up like me, a crotchety old man telling stories while trying to remember his youth. You still have a lifetime of stories to make!"

Charlie pushed Ramirez's hands away from his robe.

"The war changed me ... the war," Charlie began.

"It changes all of us, but don't let it own you! Don't you have kin or anyone? Look, Charlie, I appreciate what you're trying to do, and you're good at some of it, but until you face your demons and get back to who you are, what you do and why God put ya here, you're just riding in circles," Ramirez stated.

Charlie stepped away from the church wall and watched the sun disappearing behind the mountains.

"I was a farmer and a good soldier. Now I'm a horrible preacher. I don't know what to do."

"Well, staying here, hiding from your past with all us old men won't get your head right," Ramirez noted. "Have you looked into the eyes of these men, these priests ... some died inside long ago."

"So, go where, and do what? I was good at killing ... damn good. That's why I stayed here, to make amends for the sins I committed and to find some sane explanation about why men are so corrupt and evil. Have you ever had to kill a man for a ladle of muddy water just so you won't die of thirst? Or tortured someone and kept him in a cage for entertainment? Those sons of bitches at Alton prison ..." He trailed off.

Ramirez stepped back to collect his thoughts. He knew Charlie had been through hell, and he wanted to help him. He had seen his wounds, and he remembered how Charlie used to scream out in the night when he first arrived at the church. Charlie was getting better, but now he was just treading water, either afraid to move on or wanting to hide from any of the world. Ramirez wanted the best for him.

"Listen, amigo, they want you to go to Santa Fe. If I were you, I'd take the offer. Maybe a change of scenery will help, and maybe you can help those people up north. I think some change will do your heart good. If you get away from here, you might find your path. It's time to go, Charlie."

"Is everything alright, brother Ramirez?" called out a brash voice.

Charlie and Ramirez turned to see Father Brady standing with a bucket of water in one hand and a rake in the other.

"Yes, Father. We were discussing Charlie's ... new opportunity," Ramirez explained.

"Santa Fe is a good place to begin your ministries away from this monastery, brother Blackburn. I have known the priest there for several years." Father Brady added, "We thank you for your services and for your willingness to learn of the Lord."

Brother Ramirez leaned over and whispered, "Look at those dead eyes."

"So, I am to be moving on?" Charlie asked trying to hold back a laugh.

"Yes, but it's for your own good, my son. We want what's best for you and Santa Fe, and Father Ortiz may be just what you need. We have taught you all we can here, so it's time to move on. They expect you in a few days, so the sooner, the better." Father Brady turned and walked back into the monastery.

"He always liked me, "Charlie joked.

"Yeah, he likes me too," Ramirez said with a sly smile.

"Come, I'll help you pack. It could be a hard journey, so let's pack light. We need to find you a strong ride and a good gun, as well."

"To be honest, those are two things I do miss," Charlie said with a grin as the men walked past the gates of the church.

"Did I ever tell you about the time me and my gang held off fifty Mexican soldiers in Texas?" Ramirez asked.

"Yep, about a dozen times," Charlie answered back.

"Oh good, that means you liked it … it was a hot September morning with blue skies. We heard the sound of horses thundering down a gulch …" he began.

Charlie just smiled.

Chapter 3

The town was still in mourning. Beth had been laid to rest on Saturday afternoon in a small cemetery about a mile outside of town. A few of her closest friends knew of their love affair, and some even knew of their plans of marriage. It was a romance with a tragic ending. Days marched on as a new week began. New Mexico life would continue to move forward, and so would the talk and local gossip. Rumors and gossip spread from the saloon to the church building at the end of Main Street; everyone had an opinion.

The men and women of High Range went about their daily routines. High Range had nearly twenty buildings and three streets. The town saw a great deal of growth after the war between the states ended the year before. Folks looking for new beginnings were drawn to High Range. On the one hand, that was good for the town, but it also drew those looking for a new start in crime. The territory had been plagued with raiders, horse thieves, and outlaws for the last seven months. Even with the judge and Marshal Cole, the county struggled to eke out a civilized existence.

Marshal Cole was a bear of a man, standing head and shoulders above most. He was as thick as an oak tree and just as solid. Cole earned his fearsome reputation fighting for the Rebels against the Union army, and his many brave deeds helped get him his position as marshal. Marshal Cole was fast with a gun and even faster to put a man on the ground with his fist. He was known for being short on patience and mercy. With this reputation, townsfolk figured he'd have no trouble cleaning up the territory, but a bad element of men had killed off his deputies and made his job that much harder.

Cole lumbered across the muddy street, dressed in black from hat to boot. He wore a deep scowl on his scruffy face. It was Monday, and he hated Mondays. He also hated the winds of New Mexico and the fact that Judge Murphy was waiting for him in his office. The day was just starting, and his cold blue eyes scanned the street, noting the comings and goings of the townsfolk as the town came alive. A young girl, no more than thirteen years old, stood on a wooden sidewalk near the General Store. She played a fiddle, bringing a fresh sound of music to the morning air. Cole nearly stomped by her but stopped short. He kicked the small sun hat near her feet, sending loose change and a couple wadded up bills into the muddy streets.

"I told you no permit, no music. Now get out of here!" he barked.

The young girl quickly scurried to pick up the mud-coated coins. Hearing the commotion, a few of the town's folks stopped to watch. As Cole adjusted his hat and looked down the street, the people went back to their business as if no one saw a thing. He continued on to a building at the center of town. The wooden sign said Sheriff, but Marshal Cole had greater jurisdiction than a sheriff. In his position, he had more power town-to-town, thanks to the judge. He opened the door to the building and stepped inside. His face went cold as he saw the judge with his hands behind his back, gazing at a wall covered in wanted posters.

"Morning Judge. I see you are prompt as always," he said.

The judge released his hands, and clenching his fists, he continued to look at the wall of wanted men. He wasn't focused on them. He wanted Jack. The rest could burn in hell another day.

"It's been three days and nothing. We have searched three days. He's wounded; I hit the son of a bitch," the judge said angrily.

"I know. I have four men looking at this very moment. I've lost so many deputies in the last six weeks ... we have a lot of territory to cover, and manpower is down," Cole offered as an explanation.

"I want him found. I want his face posted in every town and trading post. I want it plastered on every outhouse in the state!" the judge demanded.

"It's a dangerous place out there right now. With the war over and people moving in and out, lots of bad folks are entering the territory. We will get him, but we need more time," Cole said.

The judge spun around quickly.

"We do not have time! He could be walled up, waiting, and healing, and then he shoots down to Mexico. Time and patience are the two things I have little of right now, Marshal. That son of a bitch will pay for killing my daughter."

Cole looked at the wall of wanted men.

"I'll send out the bounty today ..."

"I want it high," the judge ordered. "Make it ten ... no twenty thousand dollars. But he must be brought in alive!"

Cole's mouth dropped just a hair. "Twenty thousand dollars; that's a small fortune. It's a bit much," he contested.

The judge looked at him sternly. "Just do it; I have the money, but he has to be alive! The bigger the bounty, the more people looking!"

Marshal Cole studied the wall with its poorly drawn faces of killers, rapists, cattle rustlers, and bandits. "You know ... I may have a way to fix both of our problems. How bad do you want this man?" Cole asked.

"If vengeance were a horse, I would ride it through the gates of hell itself! But I want him alive! I want to see the light burn out from his eyes."

"My idea could buy us some time. I could get more deputies and clean up my wall. I bet you would have him in a week or so, but it could be risky."

The judge strode to the marshal and stuck his finger in his face.

"You make it happen and bring that man to me. I am the judge. I am the power in this Territory, so you just do it!"

The marshal's lip curled in a cunning grin. "I will make it happen ... Your Honor."

The judge adjusted his coat and with a curse under his breath, he stormed from Cole's office. Cole rubbed his shaggy face and walked over to the wall of wanted men and women.

His mind flashed back to the war. It was brutal and cold, but he never took orders from anyone when he could help it. When he did take an order, he ignored it as much as he could get away with. Being under the judge's boot was an irritating itch, but the job of marshal had its perks. Power was just one of the perks. When the judge was away, Cole was king.

"We will find that son of a bitch and kill all this trash at the same time," he said to himself. "Opportunity is knocking again." He sat down at the desk and taking quill and ink in hand, he wrote on worn, tan paper.

Two hours later, Marshal Cole addressed a small crowd outside the feed store. He was cocky as he raised the wanted poster, waving it in the air like a first place ribbon. He knew how gossip and news spread in those parts. He knew his public display would make sure the story of the twenty-thousand-dollar bounty and pardon would spread like wildfire. Everyone wanted a chance at a better life, whether it was for the cash or a chance to be cleared of any list of crimes in the state. It was a chance for someone to get a new start. What man or woman down on their luck, maybe running from the law, would not want a fresh start and an opportunity to earn a fortune?

People formed search parties and began making plans for what they would do with the money reward when they got it. Young, old, men, and women ... they looked at this bounty like a magic ticket. Word spread quickly to the surrounding towns, and so did rumors and tales about the killing. There was not a man, woman, or child within one hundred and fifty miles who hadn't heard about the bounty. The hunt would begin on a foundation of dreams and greed instead of truth and reality.

Chapter 4

Miles away in Pines Bluff, the sheriff sat at his desk with a tin cup of coffee in one hand and the wanted poster in the other. Sheriff Ryan was just about as stubborn as an old man could be, with a gleam in his eyes, and a hunger for excitement in his soul. He was widowed and had grown bored with the life of a small-time sheriff. The monotony of finding missing cattle and chasing drunks from the local watering hole had dug a giant hole of depression right where his heart used to be. Lately, his only excitement was the bandit Sanchez and his gang, who had tormented Pine Bluffs and other nearby towns for years.

Sheriff Ryan sipped his coffee again. His torment from Sanchez and his gang was over now; two weeks ago, he had caught Sanchez, and now the legendary bandit was staring at him from the other side of a jail cell.

"What is that you're reading you dirty gringo bastard, a letter from your mail order bride? She saw your face and committed suicide? Ha-ha!" Sanchez sneered.

Sanchez was like a wild mustang; young, strong, and unpredictable. He had a charming smile and long black hair that hid his crafty brown eyes. Ryan smiled. Sanchez was a wise-ass but always funny.

"No, it's a bounty; twenty-thousand dollars and a pardon to anyone who can bring this son of a bitch to the judge alive."

"Twenty?" Sanchez asked. I killed ten men and am only worth two thousand!" Sanchez paused a few seconds. "Did you say pardon?"

"Yes, pardon, too," the sheriff replied.

"How many people did this man kill?" Sanchez enquired.

"It's not how many but who. Looks like he killed the judge's daughter ... big mistake there. Too bad you're stuck here; your trial is in two weeks."

"So all someone has to do is bring this gringo to the judge, and they get to go free and get stinking rich?" Sanchez asked once again.

"Yep. I may leave here and go searching myself. Maybe I'll go see if I can find him," Ryan said.

He put the tin cup down and stood up, his eyes never leaving the poster.

"I believe you have a trial and possible hanging to attend ... mine, remember?" Sanchez added.

"Ya know, lots of bad people will be looking for this fella. It's not everyday folks get this chance. There could be some pretty desperate men trying to find him just for the pardon. I may not be able find this guy alone." He turned and handed Sanchez the wanted poster.

"You got two weeks until the hanging; I'll give you a chance to earn your freedom if you help me catch this kid."

"So you get the cash, and I get the pardon," Sanchez stated.

"There will be a lot of players in this party, and as good as I am, I will need someone with your skills. I'll give you the pardon and five hundred in cash if we get him. If not, we return back here in two weeks."

"I got two weeks to save my neck, or I can stay here and sit in a cell with your snoring and bad cooking? I'll do it," Sanchez said.

"If you try anything, I will shoot you in the back and tell everyone you tried to escape. No funny business, Sanchez. I want your word, and I want your best. This is not something to take lightly. Lots of bad men out there – some are worse than you and are faster on the draw. If we work together, we may get lucky, and we can both get what we want," Sheriff Ryan stated.

"I may be a thief and a rogue, but I am a man of my word; ask anyone who's rode with me," the bandit said.

"I can't ask them, Sanchez, they're all dead. You're too hot-headed. You got a temper like TNT and a quick mouth to match. It took me four years to bring you here, and I can't believe I am thinking about this, but, I sure as hell can't do it alone. I know all your tricks and all your ways. I also know you're a man of your word. If you weren't, your gang would have never been so loyal after all you've done."

"True. I never lied to them. They were my brothers … my friends. Damn Pinkertons on that train. You can thank them for putting me in that cave where you found me. I lost everyone, and then you come crawling around like a snake and … well … I thought you died or retired, but there you were with a badge and a gun," Sanchez said.

"I can still retire if you come help me. You can go free. This town doesn't give a piss about you or me. Most of the bad blood was from three years ago, so let's change our destiny. Let's go do something."

"Yes, we will find this bastard, get our reward, and ride off into the sunset. You an old rich man, and me free!"

"Great, now you're talking."

Ryan opened the door to the jail cell with a key.

"Do I get a gun?" Sanchez asked

"No."

"Do I get these chains off me?"

"No."

"Do I at least get a horse?"

"I'll think about it."

Sanchez looked at Sheriff Ryan. He knew this was his one chance to get away from Ryan. He could run and try to get to Mexico. He could slam the old man across the jaw and take his gun. He could find a new gang.

So many thoughts ran through his mind so quickly. There was something in Ryan's eyes, a small look of adventure, that stopped him. It was a glimpse of a wild man yearning for something, perhaps a new life. Sanchez liked adventure. He liked freedom and the open road. He could always try to escape in a couple weeks. For now, there was hope and adventure. If this lawman were willing to trust him, he would keep his hot temper and smart mouth in check ... at least for the moment.

He put out his hand.

"The dirty Sanchez gang rides again," he said. He then spat in his palm and smiled. Ryan let out a sigh and shook his hand.

"I'm a great tracker. We will find him and beat everyone to that reward, amigo. I am the best. You will see."

"I know how good you are. Let's move; we're losing daylight."

Sanchez walked to the front door with the sheriff behind him. Last chance. He could try to run, but he didn't.

"Just a thought," the bandit said. "You may want to take off the tin and pose as a bounty hunter with me as your hostage. Bad men love to kill men with a star."

Ryan thought for a moment and then took the badge from his vest and slid it into his pocket. "We may need it if we run into the law," he replied.

"True. Enough, we will not show our cards. Let's go find this hombre," Sanchez said. "Welcome to my gang."

"I ain't in your gang," Ryan said.

"My gang is fun. You'll see."

"This may have been a bad idea ..."

"When we get that money, I am going to get me a bath and a whore ... but maybe not in that order," the bandit added smiling.

Ryan shook his head with a grin. He closed the door as the two new partners left the sheriff's office.

****

The coffeepot rested on the grate, just above the ashen remains of the campfire. It was still close to noon, and the scraps from a quick breakfast along with plates and tin cups sat nearby. A woman with thick, red hair dressed in a tight corset and flowing skirt stood next to a rock holding a piece of parchment paper. Two younger women sat near the remains of the fire, sipping lukewarm coffee.

"It says it plain as day, girls. Twenty thousand for the live capture of this man, and a pardon to anyone and their gang. We bring him in, we get rich, and we can go scot-free."

Raven, one of the girls with long jet black hair, shrugged her shoulders and asked, "But Rose, how we gonna track him?"

Rose was older and wiser than her two associates.

She chuckled before responding, "No man can resist us, and we know how weak men can be. We'll find him and use our charms."

Lilly, the third young woman, was fair-skinned with a young face. She quickly pulled a pistol from her side and targeted a branch fifty yards away.

"You think we got the skills to bring this fella in?" Lilly asked.

Rose looked at the poster again and replied, "He won't have a prayer, and he will need it against the Fallen Angels Gang."

Raven got up from her seat and walked over to a tree, picking up the shotgun that rested against it.

"Well, if this is going to be our last job, we should enjoy it."

Rose smiled. "Yep, we're gonna be rich and free! Let's finish this."

The three women walked about ten feet away from the camp, and there, near a cluster of rocks, were four miners. They were tied up with thick rope, and judging from the wounds on their faces and hands, they got more pain than pleasure the night before. The three Fallen Angels looked the men over as they pleaded with gagged mouths and begging eyes. The women took aim with their shotgun and pistols. The sound of gunfire echoed through the woods.

****

The smell of thick smoke still hung in the air, its haze shading what was left of the small Indian village. Most of the inhabitants had taken what they could find and fled. Their leader, Chief Thunder Wolf, stood defiant, near the burned remains of his Teepee. In his hand was the spirit stick.

Thunder Wolf was a giant of an Indian. His eyes watered, not from sadness, but from rage. This was the second time he had moved to try to abide by the treaty he signed, but they came in the night when he and his braves were away. The land was dry, and they needed food, but their hunt was unsuccessful.

Arriving at the remains of their once thriving village made his heart ache. His mind was scattered and unclear. He wanted peace. He wanted prosperity for anyone who was willing to try, but this white man's military and these soldiers … were they sent by the government or were they renegades of the war? It could be looters and robbers or was it just meant to look that way? Either scenario only caused more anger.

A brave near him swallowed hard and then spoke. "Do you wish to attack the fort and steal supplies?"

"No. We are not the savages here. We are not the enemy. If we retaliate without knowing the truth, we will just bring more wrath from the lying white devils."

Two braves on horses rode quickly into the camp and stopped short. The horses were winded. One of the Indians, Red Hawk, jumped from his ride and ran to Thunder Wolf, handing him a piece of paper.

Thunder Wolf held it up and looked it over. He could read the words wanted and twenty-thousand dollars of American money, but he couldn't make out the rest.

Red Hawk explained, "They have this at every trading post and in every town. The wanted man is worth a small fortune. But he must be brought in alive."

Thunder Wolf looked at his small village, and he looked at the men, women, and children.

"We will find this white man and collect the reward. Let the white man feed us for several seasons. No one can hunt like us. I want three of our best hunters and trackers. We will set out to find this white man and save our people."

****

His thick sausage-like fingers slid the change across the counter. He felt like his constant smile looked fake, but the man who took his money and bid him good day didn't seem to notice.

The banker, Morris Fargo, was tired. Being Friday, the line he was working was long. He glanced to the next patron as the farmer left. It was her. Oh, please, not her again. Not today. He let out a sigh as Annie stepped to the window. Her face was dirty, chiseled and strong.

"I tried to talk with you last week, but you wouldn't see me," she said.

"Mrs. Barlow, we've had this conversation a half dozen times. You're late with the payment, again."

"I know. I brought two dollars. It's all I have. Crops are slow, it's hot, and my husband ran off. It's just me and my child."

"I know. I know the whole story. I can't help you. If you want to keep your farm, then pay us."

"I am trying, sir. I really am," she said, brushing her red hair from her green eyes.

"Look, if you give me one thousand dollars and four cents, you will never have to see my face again."

Annie was fuming, and she stood her ground. She adjusted her brown dress, and the banker looked over her.

"Next, please," he spat out.

Annie's head dropped. She turned and walked past the line of townsfolk with all their eyes on her. She walked past the community board towards the exit of the bank. She took four quick steps and then stopped. Turning back, she looked at the board where a wanted poster caught her eye. She ripped it down and stormed from the bank.

Chapter 5

It's a dry heat in New Mexico. But at noon, dry heat still feels damn hot. Charlie wished he hadn't worn his long black coat. His preacher collar was stained with sweat. Staying with the brothers at the monastery had made him a bit soft compared to his time in the war. It would be several days journey, but the open desert and feeling of an adventure spurred him ahead. His mind was less cloudy now, like a fog had been lifted. He kept his eyes ahead, always watching, and taking in the beauty around him.

Ramirez was right, getting out from behind the walls of the church just might be good for his soul. He walked on, leading his donkey behind him past the small clusters of desert plants. In his arm rested a large Bible. The terrain had changed a bit over the last few hours. He saw a few more trees and a little less rock but still, more dirt than trees.

He pressed on, his eyes focused a hundred yards ahead. The thunderous sound of a gunshot echoed loudly, and a bullet struck the dirt in front of him. He stopped and looked around, searching for the person who used a gun to say "hello". Three bandits came from a large cluster of rocks. One carried a bottle of tequila, and the others carried rifles.

"My, my, Padre. You look lost," the lead bandit said.

"Come on, just shoot this gringo. We don't have time for this. We need to go."

"No, we have some time. We could use money for our journey. Hunting a man takes money, right? We can't kill him; he is a man of the cloth. But we can borrow from him," the bandit said with a laugh.

The two men with rifles raised them, pointing them at Charlie. The man with the bottle took another quick swig.

Charlie dropped the rope and took hold of the large Bible.

"We don't have time for a lesson! Now give us your money, or we shoot you dead," the lead bandit ordered.

Charlie opened the Bible and then looked at the three men. Suddenly, he pulled a revolver from the hollowed out book and took three quick shots. The bandits collapsed to the ground and began to bleed into the desert dust. Charlie put the gun back into the Bible and walked over to the men. He knelt down and began to search them. He found one had cash and the other had cigars. He took a cigar, lit it quickly, and began to smoke. He walked over to the Tequila drinker and found the bottle resting in his dead hand. Taking the bottle, he sipped deeply and then set it down. He rummaged through the man's pockets and found a folded square of paper. He pulled it out and unfolded a Wanted poster.

He read it, then read it again. He took another drag on the thin cigar and shook his head. The reward of twenty thousand dollars and the word pardon took up most of the poster. The crude sketch of the young man wanted for the death of the judge's daughter stared back at him. His name read: Jack King. Tossing the cigar, he rubbed his shaggy chin and looked towards the east. Returning his gaze to the wanted poster, he said, "The Lord works in mysterious ways."

Chapter 6

Just off the town's street, Marshal Cole sat high on his black horse. The judge stood close by.

"I should be back from Santa Fe in a few days, and I'll bring another dozen men. I know a few from the war, and they may need work."

"I'll keep this town in line while you're away. I just hope your little pardon plan doesn't come back to hurt us," the judge said sternly.

"You wanted people looking … this will get them looking. It buys us some time as well. He won't be able to make a break south for Mexico with so many people looking for him. As long as the violence doesn't bleed into the town, it'll be fine. With so many wanted men searching for him, what do you think they will do to one another when they cross paths?"

"I understand your idea … box him in and let the wanted men kill each other off. Kill the competition, and clean up the territory. The downside of your master plan is, every cowboy and town idiot will be out there mixing it up with those desperate men. There will be collateral damage," the judge added.

"There is always collateral damage, Judge. But I'm sure with so many desperate men looking, they will find that man and bring him to you. If not, by the time I get back, I will have a good-sized posse to ride out and find him. Let the greedy folks and wanted men do the work. They can locate him, I can finish the job, and you can give me a portion of that bounty, like a finder's fee. Consider it a bonus for my boys and me. We'll get him for you."

The judge patted the horse's side.

"Finder's fee eh? You got a plan alright, Cole. You really think I would give someone twenty thousand dollars? You are a fool," the judge spat.

"I know you have it, Judge, and I'm sure you would not be giving it to some bandit or town idiot, either. Let them do the work, and let me bring him in. Finder's fee is all I'm asking for … you don't lose a small fortune, the law brings you the man, and we have a nice party to celebrate."

The judge smiled. "I guess you got this all planned out."

Suddenly the judge grabbed Cole by the shirt and yanked the big man down. The judge rose up on his toes and whispered in Cole's ear.

"If your plan doesn't work, this time next year you may be working at the stable barn shoveling shit. Just wanted you to know that."

"We will get your man. I won't be shoveling anything. Just remember the finder's fee," Cole said with a scowl.

The marshal remounted his horse, cracked the reins, and galloped out of town.

"He has balls. I'll give him that. Maybe he will get a finder's fee," the judge said with a smile. "If not, a shovel … and maybe a bullet too. Still a bit too early to tell."

The judge lit a cigar and walked back into town. He was close to the sheriff's office when he saw a man in black tying a donkey to a hitching post. The man turned, and the judge saw Charlie's white collar.

"Can I help you?" he asked. Charlie pulled the wanted poster from his jacket pocket.

"I was curious about this wanted poster. I stumbled upon it a day ago."

"Nothing to worry about, Preacher; the law will handle it. Besides, you're not our preacher."

"I'm everyone's preacher. Is the sheriff in?"

"No. We don't have a local sheriff. We have a marshal, but he rode up to Santa Fe to get more men to find this killer. He should be back in a couple of days. I'm Judge Murphy. It was my daughter that son of a bitch killed. I put out that bounty."

"I am sorry for your loss. I just wanted to learn more. I was on my way north and came across the bounty."

"There isn't much to tell. The man was obsessed with my daughter, and he stalked her. He tried to take her away … to kidnap her. When I tried to stop him, he killed her and ran off. We'll get him."

Charlie looked at the poster again and then back at the judge.

"Well, I guess that's all I need to know. If I find him on my travels, I'll let you or the marshal know."

"You find him and bring him in, and you could do a lot of good with that money, Preacher," the judge added. "Lots of folks are already ahead of you."

Charlie untied the donkey and pulled it from the post. He tipped his hat. "Nice speaking with you, Your Honor. Have a good day."

The judge watched Charlie walk away from town. He didn't like his manner or the gun belt he saw when he untied his donkey. There was more to that man than a collar and Bible. He took another drag on his cigar and strode to the sheriff's office.

Chapter 7

Charlie rode out early the next morning from town. The terrain was thicker with trees and small hills. He sat back in the saddle of the donkey listening to the sound of the woods. It was peaceful, and he was free from the walls of the monastery. Ramirez was right, and he knew it. The ride alone was helping him, and killing three bandits didn't bother him the least. He pulled the worn wanted poster from his pocket and looked it over again. Should he really go to Santa Fe? He folded it up and placed it in his back pocket. His mind got clouded, and he was lost once again.

Suddenly, Charlie heard shouting, not the shouting of battle or war, but arguing. He heard low voices in the thick brush just yards ahead. He walked his donkey faster and came to the edge of the woods. A military fort made of adobe and wood stood in a large field. There were dozens of men and a few women standing around the area. Some pointed inside and argued with one another as others just sat on the grass watching. The small group of Indians stayed to the outside of the fort watching the fighting as well. He didn't see any soldiers, and from the looks of its broken doors and cracked walls, the fort was in need of repairs. He watched the chaos continue from afar.

In the midst of the confusion, one man decided it was time to be heard, and he believed the best way was to do that was to be the loudest. He introduced himself to the dozens of people with a bull's bellow. "Attention all you bounty-stealing misfits; I am Widow Maker Walker, and you have just pulled on my last nerve!" Many of the men and women got quiet real fast.

The rough looking cowboy with dark eyes continued his speech, "My men and I have been here over three hours, and none of you are leaving. That makes me extremely irritated. That is my bounty sitting inside that fort, and unless you want to die, I suggest you turn around and go on back where ya came from."

Sanchez stood next to Riley. He knew a big mouth like he knew his own blade. But no one would tell Sanchez what to do, especially if he wasn't in a jail cell.

"We got here same as you hombre. Any of us could claim the bounty, and it'd be fair. If you want to scare these good people with your big mouth, I suggest you have a big gun to back it up!" Sanchez shouted.

Riley gave Sanchez a look and a grin, and he smiled back. Widow Maker Walker was dumbfounded.

"Hey, old man, keep your dog on his leash. No Mexican can talk that way to me, understand?"

"Oh, I will talk. This dog don't bark from the porch, he bites," Sanchez answered back.

Walker pulled his gun and took aim, but Sanchez was just as quick, pulling Riley's pistol from his holster and aiming back at Walker.

"You're quick for a dog," Walker said, eying the cold steel. He saw the eyes; it's always in the eyes.

"Woof!" Sanchez said back, smiling.

"If that's your bounty, then waltz right in and bring him out," Riley said.

"Yeah, and let one of you shoot me and my gang down and claim it as your own? I don't think so. I can wait you all out. Soon enough, that bounty will be mine."

Walker holstered his revolver.

"Sons of bitches, I'll get you out of here one way or the other," he mumbled.

From the hillside, a large wooden wagon rumbled towards the fort. On the side, it read, "Leduc Elixirs and Medicines". A man with long, blond hair and a matching mustache and beard drove the wagon. His suit was pinstriped gray, dressy but worn. He guided the wagon to the crowd of people and pulled back on the reigns.

"What's all this then?" he asked.

"None of your damn business, amigo. Keep on driving," Widow Maker Walker said with anger dripping from his lips.

"I don't mean to pry. I'm on my way to Widow's Creek. That's a small mining town, supposed to be east of here. I think I am heading the wrong way. But now that I have been insulted I will pry. What's going on here?"

Riley spoke up first. "There's a bounty on a man who is held up in that fort. Worth twenty thousand dollars if brought in alive. All someone has to do is bring him out and not get killed by any of us. He's armed, and he's good with a gun, as you can see by the three gentlemen laying in the grass inside the fort."

"Great, old man, you just made it harder. The more, the merrier, right?" Widow Maker shouted angrily.

"Interesting indeed … twenty thousand dollars you say. Well, I ain't much of a patient man or a gunfighter, but maybe I should stick around. I got medicine and bandages and can do a funeral or two if the price is right," the salesman said smiling.

"Oh, there will be funerals if these people don't scatter to the four winds soon," Widow Maker shouted.

From the trees and cactus, Charlie studied the group. They were a rag-tag bunch of desperados. Some could be killers, others just Saddle Bums. He pulled the poster out of his back pocket and looked it over; glancing back up, he saw many of the people holding the same square of paper in their hands. Everyone wants a better life … man, woman, rich, poor, good or bad. He looked the paper over and placed it back in his pocket. He stood up, straightened his collar, and led the donkey from the brush.

Widow Maker Walker's fuse was lit as Charlie made his way toward the group of would-be bounty hunters. "I am not playing with you people. I want you to scatter, or we will open fire on you."

Several of his gang placed their hands on their guns, and they began to stare down the others.

"I told you there would be funerals, and I meant it," he warned again.

"You giving last rights, or is he?" Sanchez asked.

Widow Maker turned his head as Charlie made his way past the dozens of people. His head was down, and he carried a large Bible under his arm. He stopped near the wagon, tipped his hat, and walked to the fort. He tied his donkey to a worn post and continued walking through the rotting, wooden doors.

"Hey Preacher, I wouldn't go in there," a cowboy shouted. "That's our bounty, and you're dead as a doornail if you keep walking."

Charlie kept walking.

Widow Maker Walker placed his hand on the holster near his gun. He waited a couple of seconds, then pulled quick and fired, striking the wall near Charlie. Charlie stopped and turned slightly. He moved his coat, exposing a Navy revolver; his hand caressed it, ready to draw. He looked at Widow Maker. His eyes were alive like fire. Charlie looked into the flames with eyes cold as ice.

"I know where I'll go when I die, do you?" Charlie asked.

Widow Maker swallowed hard. "Damn it, Preacher! That's my bounty. Don't test me, Preacher or you'll see soon enough which way – up or down – you'll be heading!" he barked. He knew gunning down a man of God with so many witnesses was suicide even with his gang as backup, but he also knew this new stranger was not afraid of him at all. He holstered his gun with a curse as the better part of valor took hold of his scheming heart.

"He has balls for a man of God, but he will need a band of angels if he thinks he is walking out of here with that man," Riley said. "I do not care how quick he is with a gun."

They watched as Charlie walked into the fort and stepped over the three dead bodies. He looked at the corpses faces, frozen in death, all were hit in the chest. Someone was a good shot. They knew how to kill a man. He came to a door, slowly opened it and walked inside, disappearing from view.

Inside it was dark. Not enough room for much but supplies, some rope, and old boxes. Charlie took one more step before a pistol was placed to his temple.

"Preacher or not, I'll send you to God the hard way," came a strong but trembling voice.

Charlie let out a sigh. "Ya know, for a little brother, you sure find big trouble."

"Charlie?" Jack asked. As he moved a little to the left, the dim light shadowed the man's face.

"Charlie … we thought you … the war, we thought you were dead. I did not kill Beth!" He lowered the gun quickly as Charlie turned toward him and smiled.

"I was on my way traveling to Santa Fe. I found this on my way up here." Charlie took out the Wanted poster and unfolded it.

"Where have you been?" Jack began. "It's been over a year."

"Got captured, escaped after months, hid, war ended, and I was at preaching school … a mission for the several months. I was going to go home, but thing didn't turn out that way."

"When the war ended, no one could find you! We didn't hear from you. I took a job at a ranch, moved out here, met Beth."

Jack looked his older brother over; the white collar still struck him as odd. "A preacher? Mom won't believe it."

"I thought it might be good, seeing all the bad I saw and deeds I did during the war," Charlie added.

"Well, I didn't kill Beth. I loved her. We went to sneak out, and he caught us. He just went crazy. He took a shot at me … and Beth … she …" His eyes watered, and he shut down.

"I didn't think you did it, Jack. Not in cold blood."

"How many men outside; how bad is it, Charlie?"

"Oh, about three-dozen or so. It's a rough group, too … bandits, bounty hunters, and desperate men and women. The cash is an incentive, but the pardon … well, that changes everything."

"Pardon?"

"Yes, sir, take a look." Charlie handed his brother the poster.

"Pardon to any wanted man and their gang. He is the judge in this miserable territory, so he can do almost anything he wants. Trust me, this is not how I thought to find you. I was going to come home when I felt ready, just needed more time. I found this poster, and to be honest, didn't even think it would be you … but it is."

"Son of a bitch," Jack mumbled, looking at his poorly sketched face.

"Yep, right now you got over fifty guns outside, waiting to bring you in. They're willing to kill each other to get you, too. It's a pissing contest, and you're the grass."

Jack looked at the poster and scratched the back of his head. "So what do we do?" he asked.

"I ain't sure yet. How bad is the leg?" Charlie asked, pointing to his brother's blood coated pant leg.

"It's broken. The bullet went through and did its damage, but I can't put much weight on it. I came here to heal up, and those three outside spotted me. I tried to hide out here, but we traded shots, and within an hour or so, people started showing up. I got pinned in. People been coming for the last few hours."

"Yup, nothing attracts a crowd like a crowd," Charlie said.

Jack hobbled to the door and peeked through the crack, as dozens of hungry, opportunistic eyes stared back at the fort.

"We can't shoot our way out," he said.

"Nope, and if the bounty were dead instead of alive, you'd be dead already," Charlie said. "Lots of quick guns and quicker tempers out there waiting for anything to move."

Charlie joined his brother by the crack in the wooden door to watch for any change.

"Once word gets out that I'm stuck here, I'm sure the law will be coming. They won't believe I didn't do it. I'll hang for sure."

"Well, I talked to the judge on the way into town; the lawman is a couple days' ride away, trying to get more men. But when he hears you're close, I am sure he will do whatever he can to bring you in. We have some time, but not a lot, especially with all those folks waiting for a chance to bring you in themselves. All of them claim the right to the bounty and will do anything to get it. I may have an idea, but it ain't going to be a guarantee. It'll stall them until we can think of a better way out of here."

"Okay, I'm all ears. Let me hear it."

"Just follow my lead. Don't ask questions, and for God's sake, do not let them know we're kin. Got it?"

"Sure, but what's the plan?"

"Just play along, and I'll see if all that sermon learning can win over a flock."

"But what's the plan?" Jack asked again, the strain showing on his dirty face.

"I'll think of one … we just need some time."

The small wooden door opened, and Jack was led out, his hands tied with a robe that swung in front of him. Charlie had his Colt revolver in Jack's shoulders, moving him ahead.

"So far I'm not liking this plan," Jack mumbled.

"This ain't the plan. This just buys us some time for a plan," Charlie whispered through clenched teeth.

"Well, I ain't liking it," Jack whispered back.

They walked from the fort and stood in front of the dozens of wild-eyed men and women.

Widow Maker spoke up first, "So much for last rites, eh, Padre?"

Charlie reached into a pocket and pulled out a worn and folded square of paper. He gave it a quick shake, and it unfurled. Lifting it up, he showed the crowd the bounty poster.

"Now according to this, anyone has a chance to claim this reward. So, I have as much right as any of you," he said.

"Well, patience is a virtue, Padre, and you're going to need it if you think you can wait for anyone to leave him and let you walk away," Ryan said.

"Well now, that's going to be a problem. I spoke to the judge on the way from town, and he said the marshal is away getting more men to hunt this man down. He assured me the law would be coming back in a couple days. If anyone is going to see anything from this bounty, it better be before the marshal and his men return."

"That is bullshit. You're lying. He wouldn't show his face or badge here, with so many armed and dangerous men!" Widow Maker shouted.

"Or maybe he would split the bounty and bring fifty men to grab him, plus every one of you wanted men. Now the clean-up is worth much more than twenty thousand. We got under three days to find out."

"So what are we supposed to do, just sit and wait?" Rose spat out.

"That's up to you. I ain't wanted. They come down in three days. They won't collect a dime on me swinging by a rope. There is only one way to collect this bounty, and it's going to be earned. I know a way to make it fair for all of us to have a chance for this bounty."

Charlie walked his brother to a post and placed him against it. People walked into the fort and watched the preacher finish tying the bounty to the post. He then turned to speak to the group of desperate men and women.

"It's simple, really," Charlie stated. "Everyone here wants this man, and everyone has the skills to kill, shoot, and fight … so that's how we decide. We compete for the bounty. Last man standing claims him and gives him to the judge."

"Are you joking? These men can't keep up with me. I'm a better shot and could kill them with one hand tied behind my back," Widow Maker boasted.

"You said it right as far as these men go, but I could out shoot you blindfolded," Rose answered back.

"Please, senorita, the men are talking. Make yourself useful and go make us some coffee," Sanchez sneered.

"Rose is a daisy shot, seen it. Good with a knife too," Raven stated. "All of us are good with our guns and blades."

"I ain't fighting no women for money," Ryan said.

"What's wrong, old man, your steel too rusted to play with the big boys?" Widow Maker interjected.

"I can shoot just fine. Been known to put a man on his back for having a big mouth, too."

Sanchez rubbed his jaw. "He does have a good punch … not the hardest, but good enough."

Charlie straightened up and adjusted his hat. He watched the commotion continue. His diversion was working.

"My mother could knock you on your old ass, amigo," Widow Maker yelled.

"Maybe if you knew who your real mother was!" Ryan spat back.

Widow Maker Walker grabbed Ryan, and Sanchez grabbed Widow Maker. They began punching one another, as the Widow Maker Walker gang stepped up, making it an all-out brawl.

Charlie stepped into the fight and pushed the men apart. As they broke free from each other, both pulled pistols and pointed them at one another.

"Okay, stop. Everyone just calm down!" Charlie yelled.

All the men looked at one another. It was a powder keg about to blow. Thunder Wolf and his braves just watched. Thunder Wolf leaned over to one of them and said, "Just let them kill each other off, and then it will be less work for us to take that bounty." The braves nodded with a grin.

"It's so obvious. It's a contest of skills. Like the great gladiators of Rome! It is really the only fair way with limited time until the marshal shows up," Le Duke said.

"So how do we do it? Make it even?" Ryan asked.

"You want a fair contest with these kinds of men?" Rose replied.

"There is honor amongst thieves, sweetheart," Sanchez said.

"So, we all compete for the bounty. It's that or stand around waiting for the law to show up and run most of you sorry bastards out," Ryan remarked.

Widow Maker Walker found the contest interesting, but he still felt this was his bounty. He would play along for now. Maybe scare off a few of the contestants too.

"I am good with all of my weapons, and it should be to the death! Go big or go home," Widow Maker said sternly.

"It should be until the man surrenders, though death could be an option," Le Duke stated.

Charlie looked around at the faces of the men and women, some desperate, some confused.

"If we compete, that gives everyone here a fair shot at the bounty," he began. "Twenty grand and a pardon ain't going to be just given away. Someone is gonna earn it. We don't have much time! If you want to get that pardon and the cash, we better get started."

Le Duke walked to his wagon, opened the back, and disappeared briefly. He popped back into view with a handful of wooden stakes under his arm and carrying a spool of rope. He walked into the center of the old fort and eyeballed it. The crowd watched as he placed a stake firmly in the center of the area.

"Let's mark this arena off and get this contest underway!" he said smiling.

Several in the crowd whispered to one another and shrugged their shoulders. Charlie and a few more entered into the fort and began to help the salesman mark off the area for their contest. Smiling, Annie took a stake from Charlie and walked off several paces. Thunder Wolf shook his head at the white man's madness. But if he had to beat any of these men or women in a contest in order to feed his people, he was ready to do so.

Mark J Tarrant

Chapter 8

The judge sat in an oak rocking chair, smoking his pipe. He was home, in his sanctuary. The bloodstained boards he refused to clean up still told the story of his daughter's demise. His eyes kept wandering over to the dark reddish-brown stain near the door, and the drops on the steps of the porch. He would get the young man who tried to steal his daughter from him.

It was a warm spring day. A cold glass of lemonade sat on a small wooden table, next to him. He looked at the sun through the dogwood trees and then back down to the blood sprinkled steps. His mind was a bit cloudy, still trying to reenact what happened that fateful afternoon. He was watching it unfold in his head again and again but never admitting to his guilt in firing the gun. Instead, he blamed the man who was not supposed to be there … the one who shouldn't have even been looking at his daughter.

In his state, he didn't notice the three men slowly approaching the house. They stopped below the steps. The judge looked down at them from his chair and placed his pipe on the table. He cleared his throat, stood up, and walked to the steps to find out the reason for their visit.

"You boys here about the bounty?" the judge asked sternly.

The lead man spoke, "Well sir, not exactly."

The two men behind him wore different expressions; one smiled like a fool, and the other looked stern like a gravedigger.

"Well, ya came to my home, so you must have wanted something."

"We kind of figured if you got twenty thousand dollars, why do we need to find him when we can just come to you and take it."

"Ya know that's true, and not a bad idea either. Why do the work when you can just come and take it from me. Come on then. Come take it," the judge said, gritting his teeth.

The man in front pulled his gun.

"Okay then, give it to us, or we shoot ya down."

The judge shook his head. "Pathetic … just pathetic. This is not a robbery, it's a school for a wet nurse. I thought with all the reward, at least some people with balls would show up instead of a bunch of kids just off their mother's tit."

Now all three of the men looked confused.

"I'm warning you. I'll kill ya dead," the front man said again.

"'Fraid you boys caught me on a bad day," the judge warned.

One of the men looked at the leader and shrugged his shoulders. The judge walked down the steps to the three thieves. He stopped just inches away from the two gun barrels.

"Do it son. Pull it, and send me to my maker."

"Just give us the money, old man!" he shouted.

"The only thing I'm giving you boys is lead."

The judge dropped to his knees and pulled two revolvers from his belt. Pointing them to the side, he fired, killing both men. The last man tried to fire, but the judge stood up too fast, knocking the gun away and slamming the man to the ground. The judge stood up and grabbed him by the hair. He dragged him around the front of the house as the man kicked and screamed.

Behind the house in a large red barn, the man hung by a thick rope made fast around his hands. His boots hovered just inches above the straw-covered ground. The judge held a whip and looked intently at the hanging man. He tightened his grip on the whip and cracked it.

Leaning in toward the man's ear, he said, "When I'm done, you'll beg me for hell."

Chapter 9

Two entrances, made of thin logs, were erected on each end of the fort. A sixty-foot, circular arena was roped off with posts every dozen feet. Lit torches blazed near the entranceways, sending smoke into the air. A cow skull marked the corner of the dirt battlefield. The winner would be decided in this dirt, rock, and wooden arena.

"She ain't pretty, but she'll do. Let's get this contest started!" Le Duke shouted.

A line of four-dozen men and women stood in front of the wagon. Le Duke sat at a small wooden table with a deck of cards and ink quill in hand. He called out, "Okay, step on up. Take a playing card and place your name on the card."

The first to step up was a group of dirt and powdered covered miners. These men were hard, grizzled, and hungry for a chance at a new life. An old man, twice as old as any of the others, stood at the front of the line. "I ain't too old to show these boys how to fight!" he shouted. After which, he wrote "Pops" on a playing card.

One by one, the men filed in, each taking a card and writing their names on it.

Sanchez and Ryan stepped up and drew cards. Sanchez pulled the joker. "Aha! Look, I'm the joker! Good luck for us today," he boasted.

"Great, Sanchez. Just great," Ryan said.

The line continued to move as men and women grabbed their cards and signed their names. Charlie took his card as well … ace of spades.

"Sign your mark, Preacher. Maybe the man upstairs has your back," Le Duke said.

Charlie quickly signed the card. He looked over at his brother, who was now tied to a post, just a few feet from the signing table. Charlie let out a low growl and looked back at the arena. He could almost hear his brother ask if this was his plan and if so, his plan was crazy or just plain stupid. It was buying time, and that was something Charlie had very little of before.

He walked past the line as Thunder Wolf stepped up with three braves behind him.

"Just sign your name sir," Le Duke said. Thunder Wolf took the pen and looked at the braves, unsure of what to do. He scribbled on the card and handed it back.

"I do not know your white language," the hulking Indian warrior grunted. He scribbled on it. Le Duke looked at the card. "This will do, and I'll help the others if you like."

Thunder Wolf nodded and, for a moment, felt unsure of this contest. But his hesitation faded at the thought of his people and the harshness of winter. Several minutes later, Le Duke stood on a small stage near the signing table. The men and women anxiously awaited his words.

"Ladies and gentlemen, saints and sinners! The rules for this wonderful competition will be as follows: Two cards will be drawn for each contestant. A third card will be drawn for the weapons used. Quick draw pistols, blades, and hand-to-hand combat. One side will enter the field at one end, the other side will enter at the other end. Both parties will have a white flag tied to them. If one surrenders to the other, the white flag must be thrown. Also, if someone is throwing the flag, once a white flag hits the ground, the opponent must cease his aggression. Once you have surrendered, you are removed from the contest, and your card is tossed out. If you cannot fight due to injury from a previous fight, you cannot substitute a fighter for you. I assure you death can occur, so if you have any hesitation about this contest, make it known now so that I can remove your card from play. Any questions so far?"

Widow Maker Walker hadn't said much, but he knew this was the best time to speak up and remind folks of his presence. "What about hair pulling and biting; some of the women may enjoy that!"

The crowd laughed, and Rose pushed Widow Maker Walker playfully. He pushed her back, laughing and waving his finger in her face. "Not until the contest is over, Senorita," he teased.

"We'll see if you can keep up," she retorted.

"Oh, I can keep 'it' up," he replied knowingly.

Rose shook her head. "Typical man."

Le Duke continued, "At the end, whoever has their card left will get to claim the bounty. It has also been allotted that as judge, I will be given two hundred dollars of the bounty. We need men to watch the house so our prize doesn't sneak out and to keep others from coming to this tournament. No one but the good folks here now will be eligible to participate. Are there any more questions?"

"Can we bet on the fights?" came a shout.

"Bet away!" Le Duke added. "It's a free country!"

"What if the law shows up, like the preacher claims, and we're not done?" Annie asked.

"Then we all lose. So, let's get started. Without further ado, let the contest begin!"

The men and women cheered! Le Duke drew the first card and announced, "Pops!"

The miners roared with excitement. He pulled another card, "Jesse The Widow Maker Walker!"

He pulled another card, "Guns!"

Walker strutted to the field of battle. Pops tried to look brave as he took his stance. Walker and the old miner stared each other down. Widow Maker Walker slowly slid his hand down to his pistol. The old miner didn't blink. Widow Maker Walker kept his hand near his pistol. The old man stood still as a statue. Widow Maker Walker smiled, but the old man was frozen in focus.

DEAD. He collapsed to the ground with a thud. Le Duke walked from his wagon and stood over the old man. He rolled him over and listened for his breath. "Heart attack ... Widow Maker Walker is the winner!" The crowd cheered.

Widow Maker Walker addressed the crowd, "Just the thought of fighting me brings a man face to face with his maker!" He strutted off the field, flashing everyone a glaring smile.

"Hell of a way to start," Ryan said.

"Indeed," Charlie replied.

Le Duke's tan fingers drew two more cards. "Rose … versus … Harrison; weapon … gun!"

Rose adjusted her corset and walked out to the arena. A tall, lanky cowboy waited.

"Fight!" Le Duke shouted.

The two kept their eyes ready, watching each other intently as their hands slowly navigated to their pistols. Suddenly, Rose ripped her top open, exposing her large bare breasts. The cowboy became distracted, and Rose pulled her pistol and fired, dropping him to the ground. Dead.

Rose smiled, closed her top, and walked from the circle. She waved and blew kisses as the rest of her gang cheered and giggled.

"Winner … Rose!" Le Duke stated. The crowd roared its approval.

"I ain't ever seen a pair of breasts kill a man before," Charlie mumbled.

"We just started," Sanchez said. "If we are lucky, we may see it again."

Charlie smiled, and Ryan shook his head and let out a chuckle. Le Duke flipped over two more cards.

"Ike … and … can't read this … um … looks like a symbol … what's it say chew … chow …"

One of the miners shouted, "That's our boy! Chow!"

Le Duke pulled a card and announced, "Hand-to-hand combat."

Ike was a juggernaut as he stomped to the arena. The mountain man was as tall and thick as a cedar. He peeled off a coat made from the pelt of a brown bear and tossed it to his brother Calvin who could have been his twin with matching long blond hair and thick beard. Ike walked into the arena, stretched his long arms across his barrel chest, and shrugged his shoulders like he hadn't a care in the world.

By contrast, his opponent Chow was small, barely one hundred forty pounds. The Chinaman had a dirty face and a determined stare. He moved his arms in waves and stretches. From behind the rope, Ike's brother stepped up and shouted his blood lust over the noisy mob of onlookers, "Crush him like a bug, brother! Snap him in two!"

The little man bowed, and Ike spat near the small man's sandaled feet. Chow cast the giant a dirty look, and then it was on. The big man charged with a quick step, but the Chinaman eluded the attack, striking the big man in the ribs before stepping away. Ike turned and continued raging and swinging.

"Stand still runt!" Ike shouted.

Chow turned and charged the big man, leaping over him and striking him twice in the side of the head. The miners in the audience cheered. One shouted, "Chow has the most dangerous hands in the county!"

Ike spun around, and Chow threw three quick jabs and jumped, delivering a kick to the side of the head. The big man staggered back. Chow attacked again, but the big man stepped back and grabbed hold of his shirt.

He threw him to the ground and pinned him by the throat with one hand. Chow was struggling for air but found a way and wrapped his feet around the big man's neck. He began to choke him out. The big man fell to one knee fighting for air and trying desperately to break free. But that didn't happen. Within seconds, he started turning red.

"Submit, or I break your neck!" Chow ordered.

Ike was slow to respond, but he tossed the white cloth from his belt. Chow let go, and he rolled away from the big man. He stood up, and bowed to Le Duke.

"Winner, Chow!" Le Duke shouted.

Ike staggered back to his brother in the crowd. Calvin smacked him upside the head. "First round and you're out?!" the trapper shouted.

"Yeah, let's see how well you do, ya stupid sum bitch! I couldn't get a hand on him!" Ike spat back.

"Maybe you should have shown that Chinaman your bare chest if you're going to fight like a woman," Calvin taunted.

Ike grabbed his brother by the pelts, and the two began to tussle in the crowd.

Le Duke broke up the sideline fighting by drawing more cards. "Charlie ... Ortega! Guns!"

Ortiz walked past Widow Maker. He was a thin willow of a Mexican. "Watch him, amigo; I guarantee he is quick!" Widow Maker warned.

"Don't worry, boss. He ain't faster than me," Ortiz boasted.

The preacher walked over to the arena and stood sideways. Ortiz got into his stance.

"Fight!"

Ortiz started to do the sign of the cross, but as he got down to his side, he pulled.

"Die, preach …"

Charlie drew and fired one shot. Ortiz dropped back and collapsed. He tried to raise his pistol and take a second opportunity, but the preacher was close and stepped on his hand, pinning it and the revolver to the ground. He let go of the gun in defeat. Charlie moved his pistol towards his head and nodded to the white flag on his belt. Ortega got it and pulled it, throwing it to the ground. Charlie took it, holstered his gun, and used the bandanna to bandage his shoulder wound. Then, he helped the Mexican to his feet. The crowd cheered.

"Winner, Charlie … the preacher!"

Ortiz staggered back to the Widow Maker Walker gang. He was greeted with resentment and growls.

"That man has some honor," Lilly said.

"He has a nice ass, too. Too bad he wears that collar."

"He has to take it off at bedtime," Raven added.

"It's a shame we may have to kill him in this contest before I can find out," Rose reminded.

Charlie walked from the arena, receiving a quick applause from the audience.

"Well done, amigo. You're fast, but I'm faster," Sanchez said.

"But are you accurate?"

Sheriff Ryan rubbed his ear. He said, "Trust me, Preacher, he's pretty good. "

He removed his hat, revealing a scabbed over ear.

"Damn wind. I was so close," Sanchez said smiling. "I still want more than five hundred."

"Let's see how far we get as a team."

"What if we fight each other?" Sanchez asked.

"Well, I guess you lose," Ryan stated flatly.

"Ha, good one," the bandit replied.

Le Duke wasted no time and pulled more cards. He tossed them onto the small table.

"Sanchez … Burke … Knives!" he announced.

"Time to play," Sanchez said.

Sanchez faced a miner. Both men had their knives in their hands. The miner, Burke, pointed to him and drew his hand across his throat.

"Another dirty Mexican is gonna lay in the dirt!" he boasted.

"Don't blink, amigo," Sanchez replied.

"Let's go!"

Le Duke watched as the two men sized each other up. Sanchez tightened his grip on his blade. "Fight!" he yelled.

Sanchez wasted no time and hurled his knife, striking the miner in the arm and causing him to drop his knife. Sanchez dove for the knife and ripped it from the ground. He placed it at the miner's neck.

"You blinked," Sanchez said, smiling.

The minor threw his white flag. Le Duke called the match. "Winner, Sanchez!"

The crowd cheered, and money exchanged between bets.

Sanchez returned back to Ryan, "Try not to slow me down, old man," he said smiling. "We have to win this so we can enjoy the freedom of the bounty … also, can I borrow five dollars to bet on myself?"

"No," Ryan said, shaking his head.

Two more cards hit the table.

"Next up, we have Black Jack Bob …versus … Thunder Wolf."

The warrior chief stepped up to the arena as his three braves cheered him on. He looked around at the dozens of men and women. Some looked away, others sneered. His opponent was a thick-framed cattle rustler. He had a thin beard and deep green eyes. Black Jack Bob cracked his knuckles and looked the Indian over.

Le Duke pulled a card, "Hand-to-hand combat."

"I've castrated bigger bulls than you," Bob said gruffly. He spat a wad of tobacco, hitting Thunder Wolf in the foot.

"Fight!"

Bob stepped up to punch Thunder Wolf, but the Indian warrior grabbed him by the ears and, in one quick movement, head-butted him. Bob stumbled back and collapsed. The crowd let out a simultaneous groan of shock and pain. They all felt that one. Bob lay still, blood pouring from his shattered nose and mouth full of broken teeth.

"Winner, Chief Thunder Wolf."

Thunder Wolf raised his hands in victory and walked from the arena.

"That fella's going to feel that when he wakes up," Ryan mumbled.

"If he wakes up," Charlie stated. Two cowboys dragged Big Bad Bob off the field, leaving a trail from his boots in the dirt. A puddle, from losing control of his bladder marked the trail, as well.

"Let's keep it going!" Le Duke shouted.

"Wes Brody versus Lone Eagle! Knives!"

A cowboy and an Indian warrior stepped into the ring. They squared off. Charlie made his way over to his brother who was still tied to a post. Nearby was a large, tin bucket of water and a wooden ladle. The preacher took a long drink and mumbled to his brother, "Don't talk, just listen." He took the wooden ladle and brought it to Jack, who eagerly opened his mouth.

"Do you have a plan yet?" Jack asked.

"Nope, just sip the water. Just have to keep fighting until I win, or die … or marshal shows up."

Jack took a quick drink. Charlie watched to see if anyone was watching him, but all eyes were on the fight. Jack kept his head down and did his best to talk without moving his lips.

"If Marshal Cole comes, he'll kill everyone. He makes folks disappear, and the judge has him in his pocket," he said, his teeth clenched to hide their conversation.

Charlie wiped his brow and took another sip. He kept the ladle in front of his lips to hide his speech.

"Cole? He's the marshal?" Charlie asked.

"You heard of him?"

"I knew a Cole from the war, and if it's the same man, I know what kind of man he is. What was his first name?" he asked while placing the ladle in the bucket.

"I don't know. I only heard of him as Marshal Cole. Never ran into him. I just know he is a bad man to tangle with. That's what they say about him."

"Well, either way, we will try to get you out of this before any law shows itself."

Charlie stood with Jack, and they watched as the fight wrapped up. People were passing money and screaming and chanting for more. The two men in the circle were tired and tried to gain any edge, rolling in the dirt and grass.

"I'll figure something out. Just need a little more time," Charlie said. He walked back to the crowd and joined the onlookers. He found his original spot standing next to Sanchez and Ryan. In the circle, the Indian warrior stood victorious, and the cowboy sat holding his white bandana in his dirty hands, with his head down. The only cheers came from Thunder Wolf's small group, and even they were short-lived. The young brave was met with his friends' excitement and congratulations.

Le Duke sat back at the table and looked around at the remaining group of farmers, cowboys, and desperados. The crowd settled down a bit since several fighters had been eliminated.

"Okay, that was exciting! Let's keep it going. We got a few more hours of daylight. I am drawing two!" He selected two cards.

"Annie versus Lily ... hand-to-hand combat!"

Annie broke through the small crowd at the edge of the arena and stood at the entrance. Across the battlefield, her opponent Lilly waited, as they looked one another over. Lily's gang chanted and yelled, making it clear that they thought Lilly could defeat this poor farm girl. Annie, however, only saw Lily. The Lost Angel Gang may have been a thousand miles away as far as she was concerned. The two women walked through the entranceways and stood just feet apart, at the center of the arena.

"Good luck," Annie said.

"You keep it; you're going to need it, farm girl."

Le Duke made sure the pleasantries were over before he let the match begin. "Fight!" he shouted.

The two women circled one another, waiting for just the right moment. Annie struck first with a couple jabs, and then Lily countered by grabbing her and kneeing her in the stomach. Both of them landed quick punches but neither backed down. Annie tackled Lily to the ground, and both women begin punching and pulling hair and ripping at one another's clothes. They got back to their feet with more flesh exposed than when they had begun. They circled one another as the men watched from the crowd. Cheers, jeers, and catcalls flooded the air.

Sanchez spoke, "Um. Is it wrong that I find this kind of exciting?"

The women tussled, pulling hair and grabbing at one another.

"No," said Ryan.

"No," said Widow Maker Walker.

"No," said Charlie, smiling.

"No," said Rose, the leader of the Lost Angel gang.

The line of men turned their heads and looked back at Rose.

"I mean yes; all men are pigs!" She then crossed her arms and stepped away.

Ryan looked at the preacher and smiled, "Hell of a show."

Annie threw a hard right and knocked Lily down. She landed with an elbow, striking Lily repeatedly. Lily struggled, eventually grabbing her white flag and waving it for mercy. Annie stood up and extended her hand to help Lily to her feet. Lily bent over, catching her breath and wiping the blood from her petite, red nose.

"Winner, Annie!" Le Duke shouted. The crowd cheered once again.

Lily made her way back to the crowd and her boss, Rose, confronted her. "You let that farm woman embarrass us? You may get the pardon, but I'll be damned to split that cash with you."

Lily stormed off. Still trying to keep the blood from coming down her busted face while Annie waved to the crowd.

"That's one tough woman," Ryan said. "She knew how to fight."

"Yeah, she fought a woman. Wait till she has to fight a man," Widow Maker barked.

"So, that means she won't be fighting you?" Sanchez jabbed.

Widow Maker Walker growled and walked away.

"Good one," Ryan said with a chuckle.

Chapter 10

The sun was sliding down over the small train of mountains far off in the distance. It would be dusk soon. Inside the sheriff's office, the judge sat at a wooden table reading a thin newspaper, holding a lukewarm cup of coffee in his hands. No one really remembered the sheriff once Cole made his way to town just a year ago. One day he was there, and the next, he was gone. Word was he left very quickly; the judge had seen a lot of change the last few years with the war and folks coming west.

Cole was a welcome replacement and kept most problems out of town, but he didn't travel to other towns like other marshals do. The judge liked to have Cole close to his town. He intended to use Cole and every resource he had to hunt down that young man and bring him in. Guilty or not, someone had to pay for his mistake and his loss.

He took a sip of the coffee and swallowed it down. The front door swung open interrupting the judge's reading. He lowered the paper as a cowboy with a bandaged head and hand walked in and stopped, standing very still.

"Is the marshal here?" he asked.

"No son, he went up to Santa Fe to get some more deputies. I'm acting on his behalf."

"I just wanted to let ya know, they found that fella, that guy who, well ... you know," the cowboy trailed off a bit.

The judge stood up.

"Who are 'THEY' and 'WHERE' are they?" he asked.

"A few hours ride south from here at the old abandoned fort; they're running some kind of contest. There are dozens of folks shooting and fighting. The winner brings the man to you for the bounty."

"About how many men?" the judged asked, his teeth tight from fury.

"Several dozen. I tried to get him, but this Indian, well he made a mess out of me. Lots of folks with guns are there, and dozens of wanted folks too. That bounty you put out ... well ... it has everyone looking."

"Can you ride son?" the judge asked.

"Yes, sir. I'm a bit sore, but yes."

"I will pay you 100 dollars to get up to Santa Fe and deliver this information to the marshal. I want him to go check on that contest and report back here to me. Ride hard and tell him to ride all night if they have to."

"Yes, sir. I'll go."

"Don't tell anyone else about the contest, other than the marshal. Ride hard as if the Devil himself were on your heels!"

"Right away, your honor," he said, quickly walking out the door.

The judge walked over to the wall of wanted posters, ripped down the poster of Jack, and looked it over.

"This will all end soon. You'll wish I had killed you."

Chapter 11

Le Duke looked at the deck of cards. Half the deck was gone at that point. Some of the fighters had left with no skin in the game, while others stayed to gamble and watch. Le Duke got up from the table to address the people.

"Okay, let's wind this down. There's a long day ahead, tomorrow. Get some rest. We need guards on our bounty. Any of you get any ideas of walking off in the night with our bounty, and you will be hunted down and killed by me personally."

Charlie walked over and stood near his brother who was still tied up.

"I'll take first watch," he announced.

"I'll take second watch," Ryan stated.

The men made their way to their camps. Charlie sat down next to his brother. He opened his Bible and acted like he was reading. He watched the people break from the fort and set up camps. Some built fires, and others drank and smoked.

"A wild kind of a day huh?" Charlie said without looking up as he spoke.

"How are we going to get out of this?" Jack asked.

"I don't know, but as long as we're above ground, we have a chance. Let's see if opportunity smiles on us tomorrow."

"Do you think they will figure we're kin?"

"Not unless you keep jawing. Just keep quiet. They trust me around you, plus they're occupied with one another. Trust me, the thought of wealth can cloud a man's perception. We'll just have to wait for our chance."

Annie walked over and sat a plate down near Jack. There were carrots, some jerky, and a slice of bread on the plate.

"I ain't seen him eat nothin'. It ain't much, but if he's going to swing, he should have food in his belly," she said.

"May the Lord bless you for your gifts," Charlie replied.

"You're feeding him … I ain't fed a man tied up since my wedding night, and that was a long time ago." She smiled and walked off leaving the plate near the post.

Charlie smiled back and took the plate. Jack slid down the post and sat down, with his hands still tied. He shrieked as the pain from his leg shot through his body.

"This is ridiculous; they can untie me. I'm not running, and standing on this busted leg ain't making it feel better."

Charlie didn't hear him as he was watching Annie walk back to her small camp area.

"Charlie, you hear me?" he asked.

Charlie took a bite from the carrot on the plate trying hard not to bring attention as he smiled. From far off, Annie caught him watching, and she smiled back at him.

Jack was hungry.

"Yeah, now I see what you're hungry for. I guess that collar ain't cut off all your cravings. Just give me some of that bread."

Charlie placed the bread near his mouth, and Jack bit it, nearly taking his finger off. Charlie went back to looking down at his Bible.

"Do you even know how to read?" Jack asked.

"Yeah, I learned quite a bit, and you need to just be quiet and not talk to me."

"We gonna try to sneak out tonight?" he asked, his mouth stuffed with bread.

"No, too many folks, and too many guns. Now, chew your bread and be quiet."

"Can you see what you can do? My leg is killing me, and I ain't sleeping tied to this post."

"Fine, but just keep it down. I'm a preacher, and you're a bounty. Play it right, and we may both get out of here, alright? I'll see what I can do in a little while."

There was a long pause.

"Will you read to me from the Bible like Mom used to?"

Charlie remembered. He was not much of a book reading man. He got by with what little reading he learned from his mother. The priests and the war taught him much more.

"Yes, I will read some later."

"Could I have a carrot?"

Charlie took a carrot and placed it in his mouth.

"Like feeding Eli, our donkey, when we were kids," Charlie said smiling.

"If we get out of this, I'll show you who is a jackass."

"Temper, little brother."

Jack crunched down on the carrot as his stomach grumbled, wanting more. Charlie flipped another page in the Bible.

****

Several men in Confederate uniforms burst out of the smoke as gunshots rang out. Charlie yelled and pointed to the trees. He was hit several times, and his men had fared no better. He could only lay there as more of his men fell. Smoke and death surrounded him. A young man grabbed Charlie's shirt and tried to lift him from the river bed.

"We have to go Charlie; it's a trap, we got to …"

A gunshot sent the man's head back, and he collapsed next to Charlie. His eyes looked ahead as water poured over his half sunken body. Charlie crawled onto his side, struggling to make it out of the river. He collapsed on the riverbed listening to the screams of the dying and smelling nothing but the acrid stench of gunpowder smoke.

He closed his eyes, feeling exhausted ... and then suddenly he sat up and drew his gun.

Charlie looked around and spotted his brother, still tied to a post. He looked down at the gun in his hand. His Bible was next to him. He had been dreaming.

Ryan and Sanchez looked away as they sipped coffee and drifted back into their conversation.

"I think that preacher has some demons of his own," Ryan said. "Let's wake up the bounty."

The two men knocked on a door of the small building inside the fort.

"Room service," Sanchez joked.

They opened the door to see Jack laying on a blanket with his hands still tied behind him. He rolled over and sat up, squinting his eyes.

"Rise and shine, bounty," Ryan said.

The two men helped him to his feet and took him outside. Charlie watched as they tied him to the post.

Le Duke sipped his coffee and looked over the deck of playing cards.

Charlie was still shaken by the dream but stood up and holstered his revolver. He stretched as the sun pierced the early morning sky. It was cool, but not cold.

He looked around as the remaining contestants broke down their beds and made breakfast.

"We start in 30 minutes, people, so get your coffee and get your wits about you," Le Duke announced.

Le Duke sat by his wagon and looked at Jack who was tied to a post in the front of the building. He stretched and made his way to the table.

He shuffled the cards. It didn't take much time for the people to surround the arena as everyone seemed keen for the entertainment to start. Le Duke waited ten more minutes, biding his time. The crowd would be ready when he saw them getting restless.

When they began hurling insults his way, he decided it was time and got to his feet to address the crowd once again.

"Good morning! Good morning! Come one and come all, to the greatest show in the west! We will start in five minutes. Get your guns; get your knives, and get warmed up because we got to get this show moving."

A small crowd gathered in front of the wagon.

He said, "Ladies and gentlemen, fate is in the cards. We got through one fight a piece, but with an early start and fewer cards, we will keep the fighting going 'til the last battle if time permits."

He held up a small stack of cards and then shuffled them in front of everyone. He drew two cards and placed them face up on the table.

"Ryan versus Widow Maker Walker."

Ryan took a quick sip of coffee and slapped Sanchez on the back.

"Wish I had taken a quick piss. Coffee goes right through me," he said.

Widow Maker Walker walked away from his gang and entered the arena.

"Come on, old man. Come get your breakfast," he barked. "I want this done before my coffee gets cold."

Ryan stood near Sanchez as Le Duke took a card from another deck and showed it to the crowd. "Knives."

"Showtime, amigo. Looks like fate is calling," Ryan said.

"Just watch his left hand. He's a dirty fighter. I know his type," said Sanchez.

"Dirtier than you?" he asked, smiling.

"I'm being serious. Do not give him anything, or he will kill you. I heard him talking to some of his men; my Spanish is much better than yours – I heard him talking to his gang. He has it in for both of us, so do not let up."

"I'll take this windbag to school. I've been in many knife fights before you were a gleam in your unknown daddy's eye."

Ryan started towards the entrance, but Sanchez grabbed his shirt.

"Will you listen, you stubborn old fool? I can see it in his eyes; he has a plan for you, so do not hesitate."

"I've watched him fight. I know what he can do. Just watch the old man go to work."

Ryan stepped to the arena entrance and pulled a nasty looking bone handled blade. The men squared off.

"Fight!" Le Duke barked.

The men began to circle and jab at each other. Ryan struck first, cutting Widow Maker Walker in the hand. He retreated quickly before Walker could bring his own knife into play.

"You're quick for an old Jack Ass," Walker spouted.

Widow Maker slashed wildly, but Ryan dodged the strikes. He swung again and sliced Widow Maker in the leg. The crowd went wild.

Widow Maker was angry and continued to swing wildly and miss. Ryan sliced small cuts, embarrassing the bandit leader.

"It's a thousand cuts that kill, ya know," Ryan said, grinning.

"I'll show you how to cut! You ready to bleed out?"

"Better to bleed out than rust out," Ryan replied.

Widow Maker swung and then kicked Ryan in the ribs. He slashed the old man's shoulder.

Ryan wasted no time and countered, slashing up and down, causing Widow Maker to stumble back and fall. Ryan landed on him and placed the knife against his throat, but Widow Maker spat in his face and rolled out from under him.

Ryan tried to attack again, but Widow Maker Walker grabbed some sand and threw it in his face. Ryan stumbled back, and Widow Maker Walker tackled him to the ground.

Ryan swung wildly as Widow Maker Walker locked his legs and arm like a wrestler. Ryan had one arm free and tried to cut Widow Maker Walker but didn't connect.

Widow Maker Walker slammed the blade into Ryan's gut. Ryan screamed, and Widow Maker Walker leaned into his ear.

"I'll show you a thousand cuts!" Widow Maker yelled.

He sliced Ryan across the chest, and Ryan looked down at the bandana on his leg. He dropped the knife and reached for it.

"No, I ain't done with you, old man. I'll give you the chance to bleed out."

He slashed his arm as Ryan reached out. The crowd watched intently as Widow Maker sliced at Ryan as he tried to surrender. His hand was so close to the bandana, but the knife came down again.

Widow Maker Walker took the blade and stabbed him two more times in the gut. Ryan cringed. He slammed the knife into Ryan one more time, turning it as he thrust it forward. Ryan howled in pain. He continued reaching for the bandana.

The crowd's chanting got softer. They saw a man's execution being made into sport. Widow Maker Walker pulled the blade from him and released the old cowboy. Ryan kicked and sputtered on the ground.

The crowd was silent. Their faces looked cold.

Widow Maker stood over Ryan and kicked him in the face. He ripped the bandana from him. Looking in the direction of the crowd, he waved the bandana.

"I will kill any of you dogs who try to claim my bounty," he warned.

Then, he walked to Sanchez and looked at him, waving the bandana in his face. Sanchez knocked him out of the way and ran to where Ryan lay bleeding in the arena. He lifted his head.

"Thought I had that bastard ... I ... am getting old."

"Let's get you out of here. Can you stand?"

"No ... no ... I am done ... you can leave, and no one will ever know we tried this. It will look like you escaped. You're free."

"No, we have to win this contest. You're in my gang, remember?"

"I am finished. Do me a favor. Bury me proper and kill that bastard for me if you can."

"If I get the chance, I swear I will," Sanchez assured him.

"I went from sheriff to outlaw in one week. Riding and fighting with the legendary Armando Sanchez," he said with a cough. "Ya know what? It was fun amigo. Glad to be part of the dirty Sanchez gang."

Ryan suddenly stopped breathing. Sanchez cradled his head. He glanced over his shoulder as the crowd looked on. He lifted Ryan up and carried him from the arena. The crowd stayed silent. They wanted blood, true, but they witnessed a murder instead, and that wasn't the same thing even to these desperate savages.

Le Duke looked around briefly and grabbed the deck of cards.

"Let's keep it going. That bounty is for the living ... I think."

He drew two cards.

"Chow versus Mad Man Morris," he announced.

The two men entered the arena area. Chow bowed to his opponent and raised his hands. Charlie gave a quick glance to his brother, who continued to watch the arena.

Away from the now reenergized and cheering crowd, Sanchez looked down at Ryan's body. Annie came over with a bucket of water and a rag.

"I will help you clean him up for burial, and if I die, I want you to do the same for me," she said.

"He was right. Everyone who rides with me dies. Everyone who knows me dies. I am death."

"Only you can change who you are," Annie said.

"He was a good man," Sanchez continued. "I never rode with good men, and I never talked with good men or ate with good men. He was the only one in my miserable bastard life to give me a second chance."

"Maybe now is a chance to start. This contest gives us all a chance at something."

"You are right, señorita, it does."

Sanchez took the damp rag and began cleaning Ryan's face. Charlie looked over at Sanchez as he cleaned up his newest, and latest, partner.

Annie made her way back to the crowd with Charlie's intense gaze fixed on her swaying hips.

That woman is a Good Samaritan in a den of devils. Why is she here? Is she as desperate as him? She's a skilled fighter and fights with a spirit most men do not possess. Maybe she is wanted?

He shook the questions from his mind and tried to focus on his reason, the one tied up twenty feet away. He needed to think of a plan.

Chapter 12

Le Duke was about to draw two more cards when he saw four riders coming over the shrub filled hillside. As he stopped and stood up, everyone turned and saw the riders approaching the fort.

"Are those bounty hunters or bandits?" Le Duke asked.

As they rode closer, the crowd could see something shiny on their chests.

"Worse, it's the law," Charlie said. He saw the lead rider and knew who he was; big as a bear with the stare of a killer. Cole.

The fighters stopped.

"I'll go check this out," Charlie said.

Charlie walked past the arena and through the gates towards the riders. Sanchez followed him at a distance.

"Do you think they will stop the contest?" Sanchez asked.

"I don't know, but just let me do the talking."

Sanchez caught up to Charlie who kept his hand close to the pistol in his holster. The horses slowed and stopped a few yards from the fort. Cole felt a strange kick in his stomach as his eyes met Charlie's. He swallowed hard but never showed his concern. It was quiet.

Cole smiled and broke the silence.

"The war didn't kill you, huh, Charlie?"

"Damn if it didn't try," Charlie shot back.

"You got a wanted man over there. I aim to bring him in."

"You will have him. Come back tomorrow at noon, and our little contest will be over. You can bring the money and pardons too."

"It would be better if you all just let us have him now. Avoid any mess that may occur."

"Oh, you mean like the mess at Black Hawk creek? A mess like that?" Charlie barked.

The marshal smiled.

"The war is long over; things happen," Cole remarked and shrugged his broad shoulders.

"How much gold did the Yankees give you to lead us into the trap, Cole?"

"I don't know what you're talking about," the marshal said.

Cole never blinked. He just looked down at Charlie from his horse. Charlie continued, hoping he would trigger a memory or some spark of humanity.

"They all died. We lay there bleeding out in the sun. I saw you near the ridge, talking to those blue coats. We bled, and you took a sack of money. You betrayed us."

"War is hell, people die. Things happen ..."

"The plan would have worked Cole; we had a strategy to take the ridge, the camp, even outnumbered. We all agreed on the plan, and you sold us out."

"Yes, Charlie, you had a good plan, but would it have changed anything? We still would have lost the war. I decided I would rather be on the winning side. An opportunity arose, and I took it," Cole said calmly.

Charlie gritted his teeth, and a low growl followed.

"You just tell the judge to bring the money, the pardons, and he will get his man tomorrow," Charlie replied. "Unless you think you, your three men, and the law will make a difference to a few dozen desperate men and women who want that reward. Feel free to ride on into the fort and take him. You won't ride out alive."

Cole thought for a second, took a deep breath, Charlie was right.

"You entered in that little contest, or are you hiding behind that new fancy collar?" Cole shot back.

"You and the judge come back tomorrow, at noon, and see. You come early or try to end this contest, and I'll kill that man you want. Then the judge won't have his revenge."

"Judge wants him alive. Noon it is ... and, Charlie, we got some business to settle."

"You just don't hide behind that badge, Cole. We'll settle up."

The marshal pulled on the reigns of the horse, and he and his men rode off.

"What was that about?" Sanchez asked.

"Let's just say we can't trust that man or the judge. We got to get this contest finished before they get here or we're all going to be dead or in jail. Let's get back to it."

They walked back to the fort, and Charlie looked over his shoulder. Cole stopped his horse, looked back at Charlie, and tipped his hat. He and the other riders thundered off over the hillside, disappearing from Charlie's sight.

"Are we finished? Is it over?" Le Duke asked.

"No, not yet. He will be back tomorrow, with the money and the judge. We have until noon tomorrow to wrap this up and get a winner."

"Okay, let's get it going. We're losing daylight."

He drew cards.

"Sanchez versus Pistolaro Pete. Hand-to-hand combat."

Sanchez and Pete made their way to the center of the arena. The crowd, now only a couple dozen men and women, cheered and began placing their bets again.

"Fight!"

The dance began as the two men traded blows under the roar of the crowd. Pete threw wild haymakers as Sanchez ducked and jabbed.

Pete wore himself out going for the knockout while Sanchez bobbed and moved, waiting for the moment to strike. It came after three minutes, and Pete got hit in the jaw and knocked to the ground.

Pete got back up and did the same dance. One minute later, he was on the ground again. This time, between catching his breath, he looked up and saw three fighters instead of one. He blinked, and they finally came back to one, who was moving in fast to finish him. He pulled the white bandana and waved it to the crowd.

Sanchez helped him to his feet.

"I wish it had been guns," Pete said.

"I'm sure," Sanchez answered. "But then, one of us may be dead."

"Yeah ... you," he said. His smirk was bloody but serious.

"Maybe, but that is for another fight." Pete walked away, wiping his mouth.

As the fights continued and cards fell, it was clear that they'd better be good at all aspects of fighting. The remaining contestants were eager to win.

The pile was shrinking, and the fighters were getting worn down.

Sanchez made his way over to Charlie. Annie and a miner were fighting, tussling and rumbling on the ground.

"I have a favor to ask you, Preacher," he said.

"I ain't going to quit this contest if that's what you're asking."

"No, but it would help me if you did. I want you to give Ryan last rites and a proper burial. Would you do that?"

"I have to be honest; I ain't much of a holy man. I've done a lot of bad things. This contest is my shot at changing my ways."

"I don't care. You wear the collar, and you know the Word of God! I want those words spoken before we put him in the ground, and I am far from the man to do it."

"I don't know if any of us are qualified to do it, but I will do it for you. We will put him to rest properly."

"Thank you, and if you want to quit this foolish contest and continue on your religious journey ..."

"Not a chance, my Mexican friend," Charlie said, smiling.

Chapter 13

Five townsfolk rode up on horses while another one walked alongside the group. They came to a stop as the marshal, and three of his men on horseback stepped in front of them. The marshal looked the five men over.

"Mr. Thompson, now where are you off to this fine afternoon?" Cole questioned.

"Word in town is they have a contest going on at the old abandoned fort. We just wanted to go and see what the fuss was about."

"There ain't anything going on at the old fort. You all just need to turn around and get back to your business."

"Really? I heard Mitch Peterson talk about it, and that trapper Jenkins, too. Getting everyone in town kind of excited. They say they found the man who killed Beth, and the winner of the contest will bring him to the judge," the store owner stated.

"I will have a talk with Peterson and Jenkins, and as for you fine folks, you need to go back to town and tell them there's nothing to see at the old fort. If anyone comes out this way snooping around, slowing me and my men down from helping the judge find his daughter's killer, I will shoot them dead and burn down their home. Is that understood?"

Cole's patience was worn thin, and the fact that he had seen a ghost of his past dressed up like a preacher made it even shorter.

"Yes, but ..." Thompson pushed.

"I will burn down your home," Cole repeated.

Thompson and the others turned their horses around and started the ride back to town.

"What do we tell the judge?" one of the deputies asked.

"Don't worry about him, I'll take care of it. I got more men coming into town tonight. Tomorrow we will ride in, end their little game, and he will pay us the bounty if he wants that man alive."

Chapter 14

Back at the abandoned fort, more fights raged on further diminishing the contestants' numbers. White flags flew like confetti. Men and women left the arena; some walked away with bloody hands and mouths, and onlookers dragged others away. Some of them raised their bloody hands in victory, but other hands dropped in defeat.

The deck of cards had dwindled as the day's battles took a toll on the contestants. Thunder Wolf body slammed one last miner. He stood over the man like a grizzly bear. The battered-faced miner slowly pulled the white bandana from his belt and handed it to Thunder Wolf. He raised it like a trophy as his small group of braves whistled and whooped.

Thunder Wolf was the last Indian in the contest. He had been breaking bones with every fight. Outstretching his hand, he helped the beaten man to his feet.

Reluctantly, the man gave him a nod and staggered from the arena.

Le Duke prepared two more cards as the giant Indian warrior walked from the arena to his fans.

"We're getting thin on the pile folks, so let's keep it going!" Le Duke announced. "Drawing two! Widow Maker … and Chow."

There was a short pause of silence as the final card was drawn.

"Guns!" Le Duke shouted.

Widow Maker stood in front of Chow. Normally, he would've been nervous, but the third card was his specialty.

Le Duke yelled, "Fight!"

Chow drew his gun and fired. He pulled two more shots but both missed. One struck the dirt by Widow Maker's boot. The Bandit leader didn't hesitate one more second; he pulled his revolver and fired it, striking Chow in the shoulder and knocking him to his knees and dropping his gun. He looked at the gun in the dirt and the bandit leader just yards away. He was fast enough, but he knew he could not be accurate enough; still, he knew had no choice but try to outspeed a bullet.

Chow got to his feet, blood covering his shoulder and arm. He stared across the arena at the Widow Maker; was he fast enough or was Widow Maker as good a shot as he boasted? Walker took aim with his gun. Chow reluctantly removed his bandana and bowed to the gang leader. Walker spit tobacco, smiled a greasy smile, and lowered his gun.

The crowd cheered.

Chow walked from the ring, his teeth tight with anger. Widow Maker quickly ran up to the small Chinaman. He put his heavy hand on his shoulder. Chow's reflexes were fast, and he grabbed his hand and locked it forcefully backward. The pain took Widow Maker down to one knee.

"Hold up there Chinese lightning; I ain't here to hurt you," Widow Maker Walker said. Chow released him quickly.

"I could've killed you, but I didn't. You want to know why?"

"No, I do not," Chow replied.

"You have real skills with those hands. I mean if someone taught you how to shoot. You could be a very strong asset … say, in a gang?" Walker asked meaningfully.

Chow smiled. "I have to think about it," he said.

"Don't think too long, little man. Why bust rocks when you could be busting heads?"

"I will think about it," Chow said again. He walked over to his friends who congratulated him on getting as far as he did.

"You do that," Widow Maker said. He rubbed his wrist and then under his breath said with a smile, "Damn, was he fast."

****

Charlie could feel the loose tooth in the back of his mouth. The taste of blood trickled down his throat. He staggered trying to stay on his feet as Ike's brother was staggering with him. The crowd cheered them on as both men fought hard, but neither Charlie nor the trapper heard the crowd. Ike's brother Calvin was close to 30 pounds heavier, but Charlie was keeping up with the big man.

Their eyes were locked intensely on each other, and their ears heard nothing but the grunts and gasps of their opponent.

A slow but heavy left hook struck Charlie across the side of the head, and he fell down. He rolled over, and the clouds spun. The big man took a couple steps toward him. He looked over at Jack, who was still tied to the post. He had to move; he had to fight, or they were both dead.

Charlie got back to his feet, but he was shaky. He looked at the crowd as they screamed for more blood.

There was a flash in his brain, and he was suddenly back in the pit. He thought of the Union soldiers, the yelling, laughing, the blood, the mud, and the fighting. Alton prison.

The quick flashback made him angry. He had been here before, sore, lungs burning, exhausted, forced to tread by death's open door. He had killed men for a crust of bread and water. He was their sport, their entertainment. He could do it again if it meant a chance at saving his brother. He licked his teeth and gums, tasted the salty blood in his mouth. Time stopped. Never going back, never being put in a cage again. A spark of anger, confidence, and desire to fight on ignited in his tired soul.

The cheering of the crowd suddenly brought him back as the big man came at him. Charlie stepped back and slipped around the man. He wrapped his arms around his throat and tightened down hard.

Calvin lifted him up and bucked him, trying to grab any part of Charlie's hands or head, but Charlie persisted. The big man slowly lost his power and fell to his knees. Again, he reached for Charlie's hands and arms but then reached for the bloody bandana on his leg.

The trapper's trembling hand ripped the bandana from his thigh and raised it in the air. Charlie let go, and the two men fell back to the dirt both trying to catch their breaths.

Le Duke stood up as the crowd roared.

"Winner … the preacher!" Le Duke announced.

Calvin wobbled to his feet, grabbed Charlie from the ground, and helped him stand. He dragged Charlie from the arena as the crowd continued to cheer.

"This man is a beast!" Calvin shouted. "A pure beast!" He raised the preacher's arm into the air.

The crowd cheered even more.

"I don't know what you did before you put that collar on, but if you were my preacher, I would be afraid to miss a Sunday," the trapper joked. "Good fight!"

"Thanks … I think," Charlie said with a groan.

He looked over at Jack, gave a quick, bloody smile, as hands patted his back and shoulders in congratulations. Jack shook his head and gave a weak grin.

Sanchez saw the look exchanged between the two men. There was much more to this preacher and that wanted man than they wanted anyone to know.

Charlie lay back in the sand and grass, his head propped up on his folded jacket. He caught his breath staring up at the white clouds. He could feel the tooth move even more in his jaw. He had lost a few fighting in Alton, and it may not be the last at the rate he was going. He thought about Cole and then about his plan, the one he did not have. If he were to try to escape with his brother, it would have to be tonight. He knew Cole and the judge would not show up at noon or keep their word on the bounty. He let out a big sigh and began to watch the excitement of the arena again.

Le Duke was about to pull two more cards. The stack was almost as small as a hand of Poker. He looked around at the small group of remaining fighters. It was coming down to the time they'd been waiting for.

Le Duke put down a card and said, "Widow Maker Walker versus ..."

His fingers slid to the thin pile, lifted a card, just the corner he could see it was Annie's. He then slipped his fingers around and lifted again. Charlie, with one swollen eye half open, watched Le Duke carefully. He saw the slight of hand. He must have made a killing in the saloons.

Le Duke threw down a card. "Sanchez!"

A third card was flipped. "Guns!" he bellowed.

Widow Maker walked to the end of the arena and waited.

Where was Sanchez?

The crowd looked around, and people began to mumble. The door to the fort storage room suddenly kicked open, and Sanchez stepped out. His face was painted white like a skull.

He turned to the onlookers and raised his hands. They returned the gesture with cries and cheers. The

Mexican gang leader walked to the other end of the arena.

Charlie got to his feet and staggered over to Le Duke.

"Fate is in the cards, huh?" he asked.

"I don't know what you're talking about; it's the luck of the draw. Besides, I kind of want to see that big loud Jackass die."

Sanchez walked into the arena. He took off his gun belt and his knife and laid them down. His skull face seemed to give off a cold glare of hate toward Widow Maker Walker.

Widow Maker Walker watched and smiled.

"If that's how you want to die … under my bare hands, then let's go!" Widow Maker barked.

He took off his gun and knife and dropped them to the dirt.

Both men lined up and waited.

Widow Maker Walker took the bloody bandana from killing Ryan and waved it at Sanchez. He wrapped it around his wrist. The crowd was screaming and cheering.

Le Duke shrugged his shoulders and called out, "OK then. Let's brawl. Fight!"

The two men ran full speed at one another, colliding with a fury in the center of the ring. Both men threw a flurry of punches, neither backing off as the blows continued.

It became silent … no crowd, no cheers, just rage and violence from the darkest side of man.

The two men broke apart briefly, and Sanchez lunged, diving on Widow Maker Walker. Widow Maker

Walker grabbed Sanchez's fist and bit it, sending Sanchez rolling off of him and clutching his bloody hand.

Widow Maker Walker charged like a bull, but Sanchez kicked him, striking him in the ribs. Widow Maker Walker collapsed.

Sanchez dove with a weak stumble and tackled him to the dirt again.

Widow Maker Walker grabbed Sanchez by the hair and head-butted him. Sanchez fell back again. They both staggered to their feet.

"You will bleed out like your old friend ..."

"He wasn't just my friend; he was in my gang!" Sanchez yelled.

Sanchez charged and knocked Widow Maker Walker down and then attacked with a flurry of punches.

The crowd became wild with cheers. Sanchez punched over and over. Widow Maker Walker's face looked like a tomato as bloody fists collided with his battered eyes.

Widow Maker Walker's hands fell, and then his arms collapsed to his sides.

Sanchez didn't seem to care and continued punching and striking Widow Maker Walker. He was no longer in control as the fury and anger continued to let loose.

Widow Maker Walker's head shook. The crowd stopped as the horror of the flurry of strikes became a dark reality, and the pounding continued. Sanchez kept up the assault as the crowd went quiet.

Widow Maker Walker's eyes were open, and he gazed with a dead stare as the fists continued striking him. Sanchez was beating a meat bag at that point.

Charlie ran over and pulled Sanchez off of Widow Maker Walker, tossing him to the ground. Sanchez was still shaking and clutching his hands. He let out a war cry, but it ended in a howl of regret.

Charlie walked to Widow Maker Walker and removed the bloody white rag tied to his arm. He handed it to Sanchez, who took it and wiped his bloody hands.

Charlie placed his hand near Widow Maker's bloodied face and felt for breath. Nothing. He shook his head towards Le Duke.

"Winner, Sanchez!" Le Duke shouted.

The crowd cheered. Sanchez staggered to his feet, and Charlie helped him walk to the edge of the arena.

"Have you ever seen a man do that before, Preacher?"

"Seen it? No, when I did it, I blacked out and woke up with the body under me," Charlie said.

Sanchez looked at the preacher and then looked away.

"I am tired of being such a man. There is more to life than blood and death," he said gasping for breath.

"Indeed, let's hope if we fight tomorrow, we draw guns, so it's a quick death."

"Agreed," Sanchez replied.

Charlie helped Sanchez to the bucket of water. He handed Sanchez the cup of water, but his hands were too shaky to hold it to drink. Charlie lifted it to his lips.

Sanchez drank deep and then pushed the cup away as his head sank.

"I don't know what is worse, the noose or killing a man to avoid it. I will be glad when this is over."

Le Duke stood to address the crowd.

"Our last fight of the day," he announced. "The winner goes on to the final four."

He flipped the last two cards over.

"Rose versus Annie!"

The crowd went wild, trading money in a frenzy. Le Duke drew a third card from the weapons pile and called out, "Hand-to-hand!"

Two women made their way to the arena entrances. They walked to the center of the makeshift arena as the noise of the audience echoed throughout the walls of the fort.

Rose squared off against Annie. They stalked each other like two young tigers.

"You ready to feel defeat whore?" Rose asked seething.

"Whore? Such language from such a classy woman. I think you're used to being on your back looking at the sky for a few pennies. I will put you there again so you can watch the clouds!"

"Enough talk!" Rose screeched.

The two moved closer to each other. Rose lunged and struck Annie across the jaw. She stepped back, wiped her mouth and licked her hand.

"Lots more where that came from!" Rose shouted. She smiled and looked at the remaining crowd as they applauded and howled. She enjoyed the attention.

"I'm waiting!" Annie shouted back.

The women exchanged blows. Rose threw a wild punch, and Annie grabbed it and tossed her to the ground. Rose kicked as Annie attacked, but she was struck in the midsection and thigh by Rose's boots.

Annie seized the opportunity and tackled her. She grabbed for the neck and applied pressure. Rose fought back and tried to squirm her way loose but nothing gave.

"Throw it, or I snap your neck," Annie ordered.

Rose's hands slowly slid to her white surrender flag, but then glided to her boot instead. She pulled a long knife and tried to swing it at Annie, but Annie caught her wrist and rolled out.

"I may not get the bounty, but I will have fun carving you up!" Rose threatened.

She lunged, and Annie stepped back and kicked her, knocking her backward.

"Throw your submission, or I will kill you."

Rose was enraged and swung several more times. Annie grabbed her wrist and, in one quick turn, took Rose's knife-wielding hand and slammed the blade into her side.

Rose screamed and fell to one knee.

Annie stepped back as Rose got to her feet and fell again. She crawled on the ground, clinging to her side.

"Quit moving, you're spinning. Stand still, you're ... going ... to die," she murmured.

Rose collapsed to the ground, the bloody knife in her hand.

Annie walked over and kicked the knife away. She ripped the bandana from Rose's waist, seeing a close-up of Rose's dead face as a single tear rolled down her cheek and disappeared into the dirt.

"Winner! Annie!" Le Duke announced.

The crowd cheered.

Rose faded from this world with the crowd cheering, but it was not for her.

Charlie stood next to Le Duke as the audience congratulated Annie with pats on the back and handshakes.

"That's the second time we saw two women go at it with so few female fighters …" Charlie began.

"What are you implying, Preacher?" Le Duke asked.

"Nothing … yet," Charlie replied.

"Fate is in the cards my friend," Le Duke answered back coolly.

"I think you know cards very well."

"I think that collar is to keep your shirt closer to your neck," Le Duke stated.

"Or maybe it's to remind me not to live like I did in the past?" Charlie asked.

He walked past Le Duke and peered inside his covered wagon. He quickly slid his hand to the door and opened it just a few inches, looking inside. There were bottles and cases, but on the floor tucked away, were ammo boxes and several rifles wrapped in Indian blankets.

Le Duke walked swiftly from the table back to his wagon.

"You need that much firepower?" Charlie inquired.

Le Duke closed the door. "Let's just say sometimes guns and bullets sell more than elixirs," he said with a slick smile. "Besides, I am just one man in the wild wilderness. You never know what you will need … or who may be coming to find you," he said.

"I understand that," Charlie replied.

Le Duke laughed, "We all have a past. It's staying alive to make a future that's hard my friend. Good luck, Preacher."

Le Duke walked back to the small table to address the audience once again.

He gathered the remaining four fighters to the front of the wagon.

"Ladies and gentleman, the day is over. Tomorrow, the championship. I present your final four for the main event! Chief Thunder Wolf, Sanchez, Annie, and the preacher! Get your rest, place your bets, and get ready for one hell of a show."

The crowd cheered again.

Mark J Tarrant

Chapter 15

Jack sat on the ground, his hands still tied behind him securing him to the tall post. He could see a hillside past the fort's open doors. The bright orange sun was setting slowly over the hillside. People had set up small camps. Most ate and drank while others played cards. It was not as crowded as before; with most of the contestants out, only a handful stuck around to see the end. They were either curious, or they wanted to place bets on who'd win.

If Charlie planned to try to escape tonight, there would be few people to try and stop them. Jack's leg was falling asleep. He was wearing down. His long lost brother was his only way out. He was not very confident after realizing Charlie didn't actually have a plan. He wished Charlie never found him because he had put Charlie into a mess that he didn't think they could get out of.

Jack let out a sigh and once again looked at the setting sun. In the distance, Sanchez was standing near a shallow grave, and Charlie stood near a makeshift cross, constructed of thick tree branches.

Jack watched as his brother read scriptures and tried to lead a funeral for a stranger. He did not know his brother this way. He was not the brother he had grown up with. He was not the brother that he fought with at home or the same man that had signed up to fight in the war.

He knew he had changed. He was distant and colder. Why hadn't he come home? Why did he become a preacher? What was the past of him and Marshal Cole? How would they get out of this now? Did Charlie really have a plan or would he die from hanging for a murder he did not commit?

He lost his best friend two weeks ago and then had his brother, who he thought was dead, walk back into his life. He took in a deep breath and continued to watch as Charlie put his head down, and he and Sanchez prayed over the shallow gravesite.

Chapter 16

The burning campfire sent embers into the dark spring sky. The smell of the burning wood was strong. Its warmth was soothing. Sanchez, Charlie, Le Duke, and Annie sat close, enjoying its glow. Thunder Wolf sat several feet away. His braves were fast asleep. He listened ...

"I do not know if we will finish tomorrow. I have a feeling the judge will show up early, run us all out," Charlie stated. "Cole will return with a dozen men, maybe more."

Sanchez spoke out, "So we all lose. All the fighting ... the work ... and I will still be a wanted man."

"Maybe he will keep his word," Le Duke noted.

"No, he won't." Thunder Wolf interjected. "Your government has never kept its word. My people will starve this winter, being shuffled around while your government takes the lands we used for hunting and growing crops. Twenty thousand of your so-called American dollars could feed my people for years."

"And if you win, do you think the judge will give a red-skinned man twenty thousand dollars? Will he?" Sanchez asked.

"I have to try. Even if he backs out, I may be able to get something so that my people have food to eat. If not, then I will kill him myself for tricking me one last time."

"He won't keep his word, and his lapdog Marshal will enforce his decision," Charlie said.

"So we are the last four, and we're all in," Annie said. "We fight and die for everything?"

"Yeah, I believe so," Charlie added.

"I have already lost almost everything. If I don't fight, I will have lost it all," Annie continued.

"How did you get so good at fighting?" Sanchez asked.

"My first husband. I had a good man before the war killed him. He taught me everything … combat, survival, how to shoot, how to move and how to think. Those Cajun men they know how to do it all. He went off to fight to save our land but did not come home. With him gone, it was just our son and me. Then I got foolish, thought I needed a man and got hitched to the first fella who talked sweet. He talked a lot and drank even more, and he beat me daily. I lost who I was. I let him abuse me and use me … then he put his hands on our son. That's why he is an ex-husband. I never buried him. Sometimes, even the coyotes deserve to eat."

"Damn," Sanchez said

"That was about six weeks ago. I thought if I could find this bounty, I could change my future. I dropped my son off at my closest neighbors and asked if they would watch him for a few days. Bounty or not, I had to try. Bank will get the land soon. The damn land is hard to grow crops on. The only thing it grows is a few tomatoes." She shook her head ruefully.

Annie took the tomatoes from a cloth sack and bit into one of them.

"I'm sorry; you all want one to eat?" she asked.

Charlie took one in his hand and looked over at his brother, who was still tied up.

"I think I need to come clean about why I am fighting," he said.

"You need to come clean about that Marshal, too. You are not telling us everything," Sanchez said.

"I have killed too many men already, and that marshal took a lot of my friends and other good men to the grave."

There was a short pause.

Charlie was conflicted, but his heart won, and he talked ...

"That wanted man tied up on that damn poster is my little brother or half-brother as it were. My father passed away when I was young, and my mother remarried. Anyway, that man is my kin, and I know he did not kill that woman."

There was silence as they tried to wrap their minds around this information. Sanchez was the quickest to show some fury.

"What? You crafty bastard. This contest was just to have us kill each other off and keep us distracted so you could get him out?"

"Well, that was the plan … buy some time and see what I could do. Then Cole showed up," Charlie explained.

Annie spoke out angrily, "Funny how things happen like that. So now what is your plan? Kill us all in our sleep and run out at dawn because that ain't going to happen. So come clean. No more running, Charlie. We confessed our troubles to you, and you're not even a man of God."

"I am a trained preacher, but … it's a long story," Charlie replied.

"She's right, some battles must be fought, win or lose. We all agreed to this, we have fought and bled for our causes. Your cause is not greater than ours," Thunder Wolf said angrily. "You think the life of your brother is of more value than the lives of my wife, my children, and my tribe?"

"No. I mean, I put myself here, and I guess I will end it here. Cole will try to kill us all. He's done it before, and he'll do it again. Back in the war, he left us, his own unit, to die in that riverbed. I saw him take the bribe from the blue coats. I survived the slaughter, but some Yankees found me a couple days later. They sent me to Alton Prison. I saw the horror, the torture and starvation of that pit. They made us fight for sport … to kill a man for stale cornbread. Every day, they watched us dig our own graves and fight. I saw the darkest aspects of men's souls on a daily basis. I know about Andersonville, other camps. I know both sides are guilty, but I ain't guilty of what they did, and I sure did not approve of it. I spent two months in that hell thanks to Cole. A few of us escaped during one of the fights. I tried to find some place to hide. I found a church, a mission here in New

Mexico. I found a place to heal. They took me in, tried to help me … I thought God would show me a way. Maybe find some sort of redemption … then this happened."

"Redemption is a road many men never find because they never take directions," Le Duke stated.

"Well, now we're all here on the same road, so we better find our way – and quickly," Sanchez said.

"Tomorrow may be my last day above ground. I just wish there was a way to get this blood off my hands," Charlie said.

He crushed the tomato in his shaking grip. He looked at his hand, the juices dripping off it. His eyes watching the steady stream of red. His mind wandered, reflecting, then suddenly he turned his gaze to Annie.

"How many of those tomatoes you got?" Charlie asked with hope in his voice.

"A little under a dozen," Annie replied.

The preacher smiled. He had a plan.

"For a possible last meal, ya know … that's plenty for all of us."

Chapter 17

The morning sun broke over the hillside, painting the sky the glory of a new day.

Charlie stood on the ramparts of the fort watching the sun bring forth a new start. It was beautiful. Dew still clung to the desert grass as the breeze gently caressed the trees. Charlie could sense the peace, but inside he still felt the storm.

Annie walked up behind him, carrying two tin cups in her hand. She did not intend to startle him, but he was lost in the moment … and to be honest, it was a good moment to be lost in.

"Twenty thousand for your thoughts," Annie said.

Charlie twitched just a bit. Not many folks could walk up behind him and surprise him like that.

"What? Oh," his voice trailed off, and he turned to Annie and smiled.

"You know, Charlie, I didn't sleep well last night. All your talk about your struggles gave me nightmares. I think you were just trying to get in my head so I can't win today," she said.

"I only see the nightmares; the world is a bad place full of bad men," Charlie responded.

Annie handed him the tin cup. The hot coffee warmed the cup. Charlie held it with both hands, enjoying its heat and the smile of the woman who shared it with him.

"You're wrong, Charlie. The world is a good place, but it has some bad men in it … and you're not one of them. No matter who wins today, know you were one of the good ones. Not too many folks would do what you've done for their kin … maybe to save their own skin, but not for anyone else."

Charlie took a long sip of coffee and looked out to the sunrise again. "We will see. Tried to find redemption in a holy book, and now it's looking like redemption is a gun."

"The Lord works in mysterious ways," Annie noted with a wry smile.

She turned to leave.

Charlie grinned, watching Annie as she walked away.

"You ready to die today, Annie?" he asked.

Annie turned back to him and smiled, "Nope, I'm ready to win."

Charlie smiled back.

****

The crowd was much smaller, but the people were still gambling. The preacher, Thunder Wolf, Annie, and Sanchez stood near Le Duke.

Le Duke addressed the small audience, "Good morning to all of you. The final four are here, so get out your betting set, say your prayers, and get ready for the showdown. I am drawing two."

"Sanchez … Annie … knives," he announced.

There was a gunshot that echoed from the hillside. Everyone froze. The judge, marshal, and fourteen men in long trench coats came into view. They walked with a steady march to the gates of the fort. People started gathering up their belongings and began leaving quickly, scattering like wild chickens.

The judge and marshal stood near the gates, just feet from the arena. Their men fanned out and made a human wall, as the few remaining folks scurried out the back of the fort.

The judge noticed Jack tied to a pole near the wagon. He smiled. He had him now. Charlie looked around and saw that his brother, Le Duke, and the other three contestants were still there. He growled lightly and walked towards the judge and his men.

"I told you you'd get your man at noon," Charlie said angrily.

Cole rubbed his chin.

"Oh, don't mind us; continue your little contest. When it's done, bring that man to me, and your champion will get what's coming to him. Oh, and Charlie … the rules have changed. Let those fine folks know it's to the death. If not, we will gun you all down now. Hope you win, Charlie. I think we need to finish what I started."

"I'll do my best to make it happen, you traitorous son of a bitch," Charlie barked back.

Charlie walked over to the table where Le Duke and the remaining fighters were.

"Is he serious?" Le Duke asked.

"Serious as smallpox. Contest is on, but they want it to be to the death; so basically, we are their sport," Charlie said.

"I would rather die at the hands of one of you than a lying, white man with false justice," Thunder Wolf stated.

"They got the entrances blocked. We can't make a break for it," Sanchez remarked. "We just finish this and do what we said we would last night. Winner takes all. Agreed?"

They all nodded in agreement.

"Come on, Annie. Let's go."

Sanchez and Annie entered the arena. There was no shouting or fan fair from onlookers, only cold stares from the small army of deputies.

Annie could hear the crunch of soil under her boots with each step. She stopped and turned. Sanchez stood twenty feet away. His face was stern and ready. They both held long, menacing blades in their firm grips.

Le Duke looked around.

Men wearing badges guarded both doors of the fort. Le Duke swallowed hard.

"And fight!" he yelled.

Annie and Sanchez circled one another.

"This should be fun. I got five dollars on the Mexican," the judge said.

"I ain't taking that bet. Women should be home cooking or feeding some kid with those big breasts," Cole said with a pompous grin.

"Ha-ha, or be letting a man enjoy them," the judge added.

Sanchez swung and missed. Annie swung as well. They continued to dance and swing. Sanchez tackled her and knocked her knife away. He raised his knife. He waited to strike the death blow until their eyes met.

"Just do it, you Mexican son of a bitch!" Annie shouted.

Sanchez looked over to Charlie and then plunged the knife into Annie's chest. She screamed and clutched the knife. The knife stood up in her chest, and she kicked and held the blade.

Annie coughed, and then went still.

Sanchez walked away from the arena with his head down. Charlie ran by him and pulled Annie's body to the side, resting it near the fences. He looked over at his brother and then to the judge.

The judge laughed, "Damn it, I could have made five bucks."

"Winner … Sanchez," Le Duke announced. "Next up, Thunder Wolf and the preacher!"

Le Duke glanced over to Annie's still corpse. He shook his head briefly but remained focused. He pulled a card.

"Pistols!" he bellowed.

Thunder Wolf and Charlie entered the arena. The men squared off, hands by their waists, ready to draw.

"Charlie will drop that big red skinned bastard," Cole said sharply.

"Bigger they are, the harder they fall."

"Fight!" Le Duke shouted.

It's all in the eyes, who will move first.

They both waited. It was as if earth, sky, and time were frozen.

Charlie drew fast and fired. Thunder Wolf stumbled back, pulled his gun and fired into the air. Charlie fired again, and the big Indian dropped to his knees, clutching his chest and then falling to the earth.

Thunder Wolf crawled for a few inches and tried to raise his pistol, but the great Sky Father was calling him home. He dropped his hand and gun. His body went limp.

"Winner … the preacher!" Le Duke announced.

Charlie walked over to the big man and pulled him to the other side of the arena. The big body lay still on his stomach.

"Good job, Charlie. You kill that dirty Mexican next, and maybe I can step inside that ring and show you how to shoot that gun!" Cole shouted.

The men laughed, and the judge just smiled.

"Ladies and gentlemen, the last battle. Winner takes the bounty. Sanchez versus the preacher!" Le Duke fumbled with the cards for a second.

Le Duke grabbed the card pile and drew. "Guns!" he shouted.

Sanchez entered the arena. Charlie stepped back to the center, just yards from Thunder Wolf's body.

"It's too bad … after I kill you, amigo, I will have to kill all those men by myself," Sanchez said.

"If you kill me, I'll be watching from Heaven," Charlie said.

The two men walked back several paces.

"Who do you want?" the judge asked. "Twenty-five dollars on the winner."

"Hmmm, Charlie's good, but that Mexican looks fast. I'll take my chances with Charlie. If he wins, I get to kill him, so keep your money," Cole said.

"Fair enough," the judge said.

"Contestants, ready …" Le Duke's voice trembled. "Fight!"

Sanchez pulled and fired. Charlie did the same. Sanchez fell back, crashing to the ground. He looked up at the clouds. His pistol rolled from his dying grip.

Charlie fell over, clutching his stomach. Charlie staggered to his feet, clutching a wet wound through his shirt. He holstered his gun.

Sanchez lay dead.

Charlie turned and wobbled a bit. He walked to his brother, who was still tied up. Taking a knife from his belt, he cut the rope that bound Jack.

Charlie grabbed a Henry rifle that had been next to Le Duke's card table. He pointed the end of the barrel at his brother and signaled him to walk. With Jack limping badly, they walked to the judge, the marshal, and the half-dozen men by the south entrance of the fort.

The preacher stood just yards away with the rifle still pointed at the bounty.

"Good job, Preacher. Last man standing gets the reward, and I guess that's you," the judge said.

"Did you bring it ... all of it?" Charlie asked.

The marshal tossed a leather case to the ground.

"Open it," Charlie ordered.

The judge pointed to it.

"Open the damn case. Show him," he directed.

One of the men fumbled forward and opened the case. Inside were bags of gold, folded up pardons, and hundreds of bills. The man stepped back into line.

"That could really help my church." Charlie smiled.

"Yeah, it could, but it won't. You won't see a dime of that money," the judge scoffed.

"Really?" Charlie asked.

"You think you can just walk into my territory, have an illegal contest, and take the bounty and pardon and walk away? You're as stupid as Cole said you were," the judge sneered.

"Well, you can give me the bounty or die," Charlie threatened.

The group of men laughed.

"You're in no position to barter, and I am in no mood for your mouth," the judge shot back.

"Well, I delivered him to you, and it says pardon for any crime. Seeing how he's my brother, he is part of my gang, so we get the pardon and the bounty," Charlie said with a grin.

"Really? Your brother? Shame we're gonna have to kill both of you. But by the look of that belly wound, we'll be doing you a favor," Cole said.

The preacher reached down and held his wet, dark shirt. He slid his hand down and felt the wound. He groaned.

"That rifle won't do you any good, Preacher," the judge said. "That money won't keep you from bleeding out; you're a goner."

Charlie reached into his red-stained shirt and pulled out a hand full of crushed tomato. He dropped it to the ground.

They looked at him.

"Tomato?" the judge asked.

"You're right; this rifle ain't going to help me."

Charlie threw the rifle into the air, drew his pistols and fired. Four of the men dropped, and the rest scattered. Charlie tossed one gun to Jack, who caught it in his tied hands. Charlie then caught the falling rifle and took several more shots, killing two more of the judge's men. The rest of the men took cover.

"Now!" Charlie shouted.

From the ground, Sanchez got up and fired. Thunder Wolf fired, too. Annie rolled over, picked up a shotgun from the ground and squeezed the trigger, the blast echoing its booming roar into the fort.

A deputy near the north gate dropped. Le Duke took cover behind his wagon where a half-dozen rifles and shotguns were lined up and ready to be used. He grabbed the closest one and opened fire sending more deputies running for cover.

"What the hell!" the judge shouted.

Charlie and Jack fell back from the south gate looking for cover. The bounty of cash and pardons sat on the ground.

Annie ran behind a small stack of crates and pulled up a rifle, took aim, and fired dropping another one of the judge's puppets.

The marshal and judge hid in the corners of the fort, behind barrels, a broken down wagon, and hay. There was no escape for anyone.

Thunder Wolf quickly ran upstairs to the walkway of the fort. Gunfire erupted, sending splinters of wood into the air. Thunder Wolf was swift and made his way to the higher ground. He fired, striking a man near the marshal. The marshal ducked and looked up, startled.

"On the catwalk! Stop him!" Cole ordered.

Two deputies ran to a rickety wooden ladder and climbed to the walkway. Sanchez hid behind a wall as bullets pelted the space just above his head. After a short pause, he popped his head out and looked at the satchel of cash on the ground. It was just yards away. He fired several more shots and looked for a better place for cover.

From behind a pile of boxes, Charlie fired several shots causing two more gunmen to collapse to the dirt.

Sanchez dove and hid behind a small pile of stacked firewood. He looked over to Charlie a couple yards away and shouted, "This is all part of your plan!?"

"Some of it; just keep throwing lead, ya crazy Mexican!" Charlie shouted back with a grin.

Sanchez fired several shots as he ran from his hiding spot. He dove over a barrel and fired again, hitting a deputy a few feet away from the judge. The deputy's blood sprayed across the judge's face striking him in the right eye, leaving him momentarily blinded.

"Son of a bitch!" the judge screamed in frustration. He wiped his eye and ducked down behind the wagon. "You want a gunfight!?"

The judge pulled both his pistols and ran out. He fired both guns at Sanchez who rolled and took cover as the bullets chewed up the wood around him.

The judge raised his guns again and fired several shots at Thunder Wolf on the walkway and struck him in the leg. Thunder Wolf dropped his rifle and stumbled.

"Kill them now!" the judge screamed.

Thunder Wolf got to his feet as two men with guns drawn closed in. He pulled a knife from his buckskin boot.

The two men laughed at him.

"You brought a knife to a gunfight, Chief?" the taller man asked.

Thunder Wolf threw the knife, hitting one of the men in the shoulder. He reached behind his back and pulled a small pistol from his belt; he fired and dropped the other deputy as well.

"No. I brought both," he answered. With a limp, Thunder Wolf ran awkwardly past their dead bodies to the end of the walkway, his leg seeping blood with every step.

Marshal Cole ran from his place of cover. He saw Annie take aim again with the shotgun, and he fired. He hit her, and the bullet took her to the ground. Annie screamed, dropped the shotgun and crawled behind the stacked crates. Charlie ran to her. He fired several shots causing the marshal to fall back. When he made it to Annie, she was lying still.

"Annie … Annie," he spoke, softly.

She opened her eyes and looked at her shoulder. It was bloody. She gritted her teeth angrily.

"I ain't hit bad," she said stubbornly. "I'm a woman who has given birth. This ain't pain and sure as shit ain't bleeding."

"Cole was never a good shot," Charlie said.

Annie sat up, and blood trickled down her arm.

"Damn tomato's messing up my aim!" she shouted. She reached into her shirt, pulled the tomatoes from her bra, and tossed them to the ground. Her shirt was now stained with blood and tomato juice. Grabbing the shotgun, she walked out shooting. Another lawman fell.

Two more cowboys opened fire. Annie took cover, running and crashing through the door of a small storage shed.

Three men fired at the small building. Sanchez opened fire and hit one of them. They turned to fire at Sanchez, but Thunder Wolf jumped from overhead, knocking them to the ground. The Indian warrior fired two shots, killing the men, and dove into the shed with Annie.

Jack watched from behind Le Duke's wagon.

Le Duke continued his cover fire. A dozen dead men were scattered around the fort. Thunder Wolf fired several shots from the small building causing the remaining gunmen to fall back. Charlie took cover next to his brother.

"You ready to finish this?" Charlie asked.

"Just let me have the judge," Jack said and fired two more shots.

"You fast enough for that old man?"

"Just give me another gun!"

Sanchez fired several more shots dropping a cowboy near the marshal.

The judge looked around ... his posse was getting smaller.

"Cole, get that satchel, we're getting out now!" he yelled.

"Get the satchel!" Cole ordered.

One of the judge's men made a run for it. He was hit by gunfire and dropped dead before he got the satchel.

The judge grabbed the other man by the arm and said, "Listen, you half-wit. I want cover fire on that shed now!"

The deputy took aim as the judge ran back toward the entrance. Two deputies followed close behind firing as they went.

Sanchez fired and killed one of the men, but the judge slipped out the entranceway, firing his pistol as he fled.

Jack ran with a limp, killing another man and heading out of the fort.

Marshal Cole was left with two men. He looked at the entrance ... he had a chance. His eyes darted from the satchel to the entrance of the fort.

Annie was reloading. She and Thunder Wolf walked from the shed with guns drawn, firing at the remaining two deputies near the marshal. Cole made a break for the fort's entrance.

"Cole!" Charlie called out.

Cole stopped and looked over his shoulder.

Charlie stood near the satchel and asked, "You forget something?"

Cole smiled and answered, "Nope."

"I thought you wanted to settle up?" Charlie asked with a slick grin.

"Can you give me one damn reason why you just won't die?" Cole spat out angrily.

"I'll give you six reasons," Charlie stated and raised his pistol.

Cole grit his teeth and raised his gun to fire, but Charlie beat him to the punch. Cole was struck several times and collapsed. He slid slowly down the wall dropping his revolver from nerveless fingers. Bright red blood left a streak behind him on the fort wall.

Charlie walked over to where Cole was bleeding out. With his gun still fixed on Cole, he bent down and kicked the gun away from Cole's trembling hand.

Cole coughed and groaned.

"Okay then, do it. Finish me," he said as he spat blood.

Charlie raised his gun and fired. It clicked … no more bullets.

"Ya know, I don't think you're worth another bullet. I think you need to bleed out slow and die like your men did in the creek bed," Charlie stated.

Charlie walked away as Cole continued groaning and sputtering blood. His large head fell forward, and his breaths came in short bubbly bursts.

"Charlie, you're a bastard."

The preacher stopped and grabbed a shotgun from the ground. He walked over to Cole and raised the weapon.

"Yeah, a bastard above ground," he answered.

He pulled the trigger, and Cole's chest ripped open. With a quick garbled shout, Cole's body went still.

"I would bury you, but like a friend once said … even the coyotes deserve to eat."

Charlie made his way to the satchel. It was still sitting in the middle of the arena. A thin, cold smile curled his lips.

Chapter 18

The judge leaned against a willow tree. His leg bled as he reloaded his gun. He knew Jack was coming soon. They say the wounded deer jumps the highest, and he was determined not to let this end in his death.

The judge scanned the landscape. His eyes burned from sweat. He wiped them quickly and narrowed his stern gaze.

"Son of a bitch … I will bring the army on you and butcher you all," he shouted.

Jack staggered into view.

"You leave an easy trail, bleeding everywhere," Jack said.

"You're a dead man … you, your brother, and your friends. I'll kill all of you!" the judge bellowed.

"I loved your daughter, and you took her from me. She loved me, and you killed her," Jack answered.

"You were never good enough for her ... no one was, not even Cole. You had no right to speak to her. She was above you. She deserved so much more."

"She didn't deserve to die!" Jack yelled.

The judge shouted back, "You killed her damn it! You were going to take her from me ... a dirty, broke, ranch hand! I had dreams for her, and you took that away!" The judge all but sobbed in frustrated rage.

"You pulled the trigger. You killed her. She loved me and took the bullet for me. You're a coward!" Jack shot back.

"You're nothing to me! I am a judge. I decide who lives and who dies!"

"Not today," Jack said.

The judge stepped from behind the tree with his gun drawn and ready.

Jack opened fire, striking the judge. The judge stumbled back and dropped his gun.

Jack limped to where the judge lay and grabbed the gun. He placed it to the judge's head.

"Do it, you poor son of a bitch!" the judge commanded.

Jack leaned in close and said, "If I kill you, it'll look like I did kill her. No ... you will live and know that you killed the one thing in this world you loved more than yourself. I want you to live in that big house all alone, with her memories around you. People will learn the truth about how the judge killed his own daughter and blamed an innocent man. You will be found guilty ... not by the so-called law, but in the hearts of men. You can live with that the rest of your days. The world will know that you're too much of a coward to face your mistake. You have a great life, Your Honor."

The judge fell back. He knew now that no gun or money would erase the truth. The lie was over. He looked up at the sky and thought of his daughter once again. He began to weep.

Jack walked back into the brush. He stopped, turned and watched the judge bleed and weep. Jack smiled and began to make his way back to the fort.

Chapter 19

The satchel sat in the middle of the fort as Charlie, Thunder Wolf, Annie, and Sanchez looked it over.

"That's a lot of money," Sanchez remarked.

"Yes, indeed," Thunder Wolf grunted, his eyes still gazing at the pile inside the satchel.

"Well, last man standing claims the bounty right?" Charlie asked.

They looked around at all the dead men and then back down at the cash and gold.

"Looks like a draw," Charlie announced.

Suddenly they all pulled their pistols and pointed them at each other. Well … everyone except Annie. She stayed still, smiling, and looking at the three men with guns only pointed at themselves.

It got quiet. They started smiling, then laughing. They lowered their guns.

"I had you, Charlie," Sanchez said.

"Keep dreaming," Charlie replied.

"I had you dead, Mexican," Thunder Wolf stated.

"Typical … you all drew on each other but forgot about the woman. You men are all the same. You want a woman in the kitchen, but a real man wants a woman in the bedroom," Annie said with a grin. "I think I would have won it all without firing a shot."

The men looked at Annie, surprised by her statement. But she was right on both counts.

"I guess we will wait for another chance to see who is the best after we split this up," Charlie said with a big smile.

Chapter 20

Charlie walked past Cole's body. He stopped and gave it a glance, just to make sure. He pulled his revolver and fired a shot into Cole's chest.

He could smell the smoke in the air, reminding him of the war. It faded quickly. A quick spit of tobacco hit the corpse. A snort came from the preacher.

There were a dozen bodies scattered around the fort … men who chose the wrong side. Broken crates, barrels, worn ropes, and a few playing cards lay in the dirt and weed covered arena. There was a small war here … a war of right and wrong, and for now, Charlie was on the winning side.

He walked through the front door of the fort and found a horse tied to a small tree. He untied it and jumped into the saddle.

Charlie rode around the fort and found Jack, Sanchez, and Thunder Wolf on horseback.

"Was he still alive?" Jack asked with a smirk.

"No, but knowing what kind of man he was, I didn't want to take any chances," Charlie said.

"Feel better?" Sanchez asked.

"Yeah, much better," Charlie replied.

"I thought vengeance was mine sayeth the Lord?" Jack remarked.

"It was not vengeance, it was justice. I am making peace with my Maker."

Thunder Wolf smiled and lifted a medium-sized leather pouch from his brown and white pinto. He said, "This bounty will feed my people for several winters. I will pray to Father Sky to watch over you white devils on your journey."

"What? What about me?" Sanchez asked.

"I do not think anyone can help you." He smiled.

"You may be right about that," Sanchez said.

"You take care, Preacher. I think your bloody hands are now cleansed by redemption," Thunder Wolf said.

"Time will tell," Charlie answered.

The Indian warrior nodded and rode off. His tribe, his family, would be well fed for many seasons.

Chapter 21

The same rude bank teller was making change. He handed it to a bearded man wearing a dirty black suit. The teller smiled weakly as the customer left.

"Next?" he called out.

He wasn't paying attention; he was just waiting until it was time to close the doors for the day. He looked up, expecting to see another dull face.

Annie stepped to the window. Her strawberry blonde hair was curled, and her makeup and full red lips screamed rich wife or mistress. He froze, staring at her. He wondered ... was she possibly a model, too top-rail to be a dancing girl? He searched his memory, trying to recall when, or if, he had seen this beauty before. Her fancy green dress and large wild hat, she just had to be a woman of power and influence. The banker's face went blank with sudden near recognition. He knew her, but he didn't remember from where. Who was this beautiful and sophisticated woman?

Annie sat a stack of bills on the counter and then added a nickel.

"That's one thousand dollars and five cents," she said proudly.

The banker looked at Annie. He glanced down at the money and then looked back at her.

"Now, why don't you give me back my change, so I never have to see your face again," she said.

He remembered her at that moment.

Annie held out her white-gloved hand awaiting the change due her with a smirk on her pretty face. He swallowed hard and realized his mistake, who she was, and knew what change she was waiting for. With a trembling hand, he placed a penny in her gloved palm. She was cashing out and taking her land and newfound wealth with her. She smiled, closed her hand, and said nothing as she turned and left.

Outside, Annie emerged from the bank's twin doors with her head held high. Men leered and pointed as she strolled down the wooden walkway …

None of them wanted her in the kitchen.

Chapter 22

Jack knelt down in front of the stone cross that marked the grave. His hat rested in his left hand. He was saying goodbye to Beth … his Beth. The only woman he knew that had made him feel like he didn't have to be someone else or prove his worth. She loved him for who he was, and that was hard to find in this world.

He took a small cluster of wild flowers, simple colors of blue, green, and white bound with a thin piece of leather, and placed them in front of the grave marker.

"I will cherish all we had … for as little as we got to hold onto it. You were a great woman, Beth. I will miss you every day. I love you."

He stood up, his mind flashing back to his last time he held her. He remembered the fear and the confusion. Last memories sometimes need to be replaced with other memories to give a man strength.

He thought about how she laughed at his jokes …
and that time when she took his hand, and they agreed
to elope.

He stood up, gritted his teeth, and placed his tan hat
back on his head. He looked over to his brother and
Sanchez, they were waiting on horseback just outside the
worn cemetery fence.

He left the gravesite and walked to his horse.

"Now what, big brother?" Jack asked.

"I am thinking Mexico," Charlie said.

"That's the one place I'm not wanted," Sanchez
replied.

"Really?" Jack asked.

"Yeah, my wife threw me out!"

"I was thinking maybe go south and start a church,"
Charlie said, adjusting his white collar.

"What about a saloon?" Jack suggested.

"A brothel?" Sanchez added.

"Not a brothel …" Charlie grunted.

A wagon pulled up. Le Duke tipped his hat with a
nod. "Did I hear the word Mexico?" he asked with a
great smile.

"Yeah. Starting a church. Sanchez is our translator,"
Charlie joked.

"No, we're opening a saloon-slash-brothel," Sanchez
announced.

Charlie rolled his eyes.

"Well, gentlemen, I happen to be traveling south
with two hundred dollars, and I'm looking for a new
business opportunity," Le Duke answered.

"The more, the merrier," Charlie said.

They rode south as the sun crested across the majestic mountains ahead.

"I can see it now … thirsty, tired, in need of a rest or drink. Come on down to the Dirty Sanchez. Best drinks in Mexico." Sanchez beamed.

"Yeah, about that name …" Charlie said.

Charlie pulled out a small piece of paper and looked it over. It read Grand View Farm with directions … "If you ever want coffee. Don't be a stranger." Annie.

He smiled, folded it up, and slid it back into his coat.

The four travelers began their new adventure as they rode on in the glow of the New Mexico sunset.

The End

Mark J Tarrant

About the Author

Mark Tarrant is a Loco Gringo who loves the history of the west, and the unexplained — monsters, rifles, cowboys, vampires, UFOs and things that go bump in the night.

Writing, creating and thinking of new ways to tell stories, he finds himself star gazing at the evening skies in New Mexico, smoking a good cigar and listening to classical Spanish guitar… or Pantera depending on the story he has running through his skull.

A recent transplant to the southwest, he enjoys taking in the cultures and historic sites here in New Mexico. He has become addicted to green chile and puts it on everything. A big fan of Clint Eastwood films and comic books with Stephen King, Robert E Howard and Phillip K Dick as his influencers.

He writes smash 'em up adventures for fun and entertainment. He enjoys time with his wife and daughter and hanging out with other creative types whether it's on the set being an extra in films and TV or hanging out at the local comic shop talking to fellow writers and artists.

Mark enjoys motivating others to write, draw and create. He is the last person to hold back his opinion, but the first person in line for seconds at a barbeque.

Anything else? Oh, wait he's got another wild idea for a story… time for a cigar amigos!

You can find out more about Mark and his endeavors at the following websites:

> **www.MarkTarrant.com**
> **www.TheDeadWalker.com**
> **www.TalesOfTheDeathRiders.com**
> **www.TheBloodRider.com**